Power too strong to contain . . .

"Clio!" I yelled, shaking my hands, which were locked in hers. "Clio!" I pulled back as hard as I could, knocking us both to one side, and all of a sudden we were lying on the ground in Clio's backyard. I'd broken the spell. It was nighttime, the sky above me dark and speckled with stars and . . . sparks, flying upward? I jumped to my feet.

"Oh God, Clio!" I yelled, looking past her. I grabbed her shoulder and shook her—she hadn't sat up yet. Now she blinked slowly, looking at me like I was a stranger.

"Clio! Get up! The house is on fire!" I shouted, shaking her hard enough to rattle her bones. With the next breath she seemed to awaken, sitting up quickly and looking around her. She gasped and put her hand over her mouth, as horrified as I was.

This time we hadn't gotten thrown across a room.

We'd started a fire that had leaped away from us, and our house, my new home, was ablaze.

Book One: *A Chalice of Wind*
Book Two: *A Circle of Ashes*
Book Three: *A Feather of Stone*
Book Four: *A Necklace of Water*

BALEFIRE

BOOK TWO

A CIRCLE OF ASHES

CATE TIERNAN

Balefire 2: A Circle of Ashes

RAZORBILL

Published by the Penguin Group
Penguin Young Readers Group
345 Hudson Street, New York, New York 10014, U.S.A.
Penguin Group (USA) Inc., 375 Hudson Street, New York, New York 10014, U.S.A.
Penguin Books Canada Ltd, 10 Alcorn Avenue, Toronto, Ontario, Canada M4V 3B2
(a division of Pearson Penguin Canada, Inc.)
Penguin Books Ltd, 80 Strand, London WC2R 0RL, England
Penguin Ireland, 25 St Stephen's Green, Dublin 2, Ireland
(a division of Penguin Books Ltd)
Penguin Group (Australia), 250 Camberwell Road, Camberwell,
Victoria 3124, Australia (a division of Pearson Australia Group Pty Ltd)
Penguin Books India Pvt Ltd, 11 Community Centre, Panchsheel Park,
New Delhi - 110 017, India
Penguin Group (NZ), Cnr Airborne and Rosedale Roads, Albany,
Auckland 1310, New Zealand (a division of Pearson New Zealand Ltd)
Penguin Books (South Africa) (Pty) Ltd, 24 Sturdee Avenue,
Rosebank, Johannesburg 2196, South Africa

Penguin Books Ltd, Registered Offices: 80 Strand, London WC2R 0RL, England

10 9 8 7 6 5 4 3 2 1

Interior design by Christopher Grassi

Library of Congress Cataloging-in-Publication Data is available

Printed in the United States of America

With many thanks to the real Melya,
for all you've done

"Here." I pushed the cookies over to Thais. "Crumble them on top. It's good."

Thais took a couple of cookies and dutifully crumbled them over her ice cream. Then she took a bite and nodded. "'S good."

We kept up the everything's-normal ice cream eating for another two minutes, and then at the exact same time, we put down our spoons and stared at each other.

"Immortal," said Thais.

"Yeah. If we believe them." I had a sudden thought. Quickly I ran upstairs to my room and pulled out an old photo album. I brought it downstairs and opened it on the kitchen table between us. Together Thais and I looked at pictures from when I was way little, a baby, and on up till when I was about three. I was an extremely pretty baby.

Nan—Petra—looked exactly the same as she did today. She hadn't aged a bit in seventeen years. And I, with my razor-sharp skills of observation, had never noticed it. She'd always just been Nan. I was trying to process the knowledge that she was so much more than she'd ever told me.

"So," I said, closing the book with a sigh, "they were probably telling the truth. Or mostly."

Thais nodded. "I'm totally freaking."

I gave a short laugh. "That's one word for it." I sighed. I was having a rough summer, and so far, I had no signs that anything was going to get easier.

"Just all of it," said Thais. "Twins." She pointed at me, then at herself, summing up the whole, huge, identical-twins-separated-at-birth thing with one gesture. "Luc." She closed her eyes and breathed out heavily, summing up the whole, huge, two-timing-lying-bastard-witch-boyfriend thing. "Witches." She shook her head slowly about the whole, huge, finding-out-you're-a-witch-and-so-is-your-family thing.

"And now the possibility of being immortal," I said. "Oh, and almost being killed a bunch of times."

"It's been a crazed couple of months," Thais said, and that reminded me that on top of everything else, she'd lost her father—our father—just this summer. Even though I'd never known him, I still felt pangs of loss, so I could barely imagine what she had to be going through.

"Been a roller-coaster ride," I agreed.

"So what now?" Thais asked. "It's all too much. I don't know where to start."

I thought for a minute. Usually I left the dealing with stuff to my not-grandmother, Petra. Nan. I mean, I'd always thought she was my grandmother. She'd said she was. She'd raised me after my mother died giving birth to me and my surprise sister. But as it turned out, she was an *ancestor*, a great-grandmother so many times back that I couldn't even put in enough *greats*. And she'd kept my sister and my dad a secret from me. I could have known them both all this time. Now he was dead and my chance was gone. I still couldn't believe Nan had done it, no matter what her reasons were. And I had missed growing up with a sister.

Now Nan was who knew where, and I didn't know when or if she was coming back. If she wasn't back by midnight on Wednesday, I was supposed to open a spelled cabinet in the workroom and find instructions there. In the meantime, I had to handle everything.

"Okay, so the Treize," I said, sitting down and taking another swipe at my ice cream. "They want us to complete their coven so they can do the big schmancy spell that will blow everyone's minds with power."

"*Is* there a spell like that?" Thais asked. "Where everyone would get power and then be able to use it for whatever they want?"

"I don't know. I guess they think there is. I don't know how it would work or what it would do to them or us."

"Besides make us immortal," said Thais.

"Well, yeah, besides that. So they say. I've never heard of anything like that."

"Luc said he wanted to die," Thais said, not looking at me. "That he was tired of immortality and wanted to die."

Luc. Would I ever not flinch when I heard his name? Luc-Andre. I'd known him as Andre. Thais had known him as Luc. Each of us had gone out with him, kissed him, fallen in love with him. He had betrayed us twice: first with each other and then by being one of the Treize. Even now, with my rage still burning, some part inside me ached for him, longed for him, wished he could be mine. Mine and not Thais's.

But he loved *her*.

I swallowed hard. "Yeah. I'm willing to give him a hand with that."

Thais gave me a wry look, then her face sobered. "Do you think he means it?"

I looked back at her. "Do you care?"

She turned away and didn't answer.

I took a deep breath and pushed my bowl away. "Would you want immortality?"

"I don't know."

"We have to figure this stuff out. Like, now we've met all of them. Who in the Treize is trying to kill us?"

"If it *is* someone from the Treize. We don't know that for sure," Thais pointed out.

"Well, no," I agreed. "But they're the obvious place to start. I mean, the attacks had magick behind them." Someone had been trying to hurt both me and Thais ever since she moved to New Orleans. At first it had seemed like "accidents," but then when whoever it was finally came after us both together with an angry mass of wasps, we realized there had to be a connection with all the other near misses.

"Yeah, you're right. Okay, then. Someone from the Treize. Not Petra," said Thais.

"No. Not Axelle or Daedalus or Jules," I added, naming three witches we'd just met. "They've had plenty of clear shots at you." Thais had been living at Axelle's since her—our—dad had died.

"And not Ouida. I hope." Thais looked troubled. "I really liked her. But I just couldn't face dinner with her . . . after all that."

"No. And Sophie and Manon just got to town," I said. "So we can rule them out."

"And the ones who aren't here, what, Marcel? And . . . Claire? Not them."

I nodded, then got up and grabbed a sheet of paper and a pen. I made a list of everyone we had put in the not-guilty category. "Who's left?"

Thais thought. "You and me. Richard," she said, pronouncing his name Ree-shard. "Luc."

"Richard was around Axelle's a lot too, wasn't he? So probably not him. And *we're* not doing it," I said. I looked at the paper. Only Luc left, which was impossible. Unbelievable. Probably. "Wait—what if Axelle, Jules, Richard, or Daedalus didn't try to kill you at Axelle's because it would have been too obvious? That doesn't necessarily put them in the clear."

"But Axelle is the one who saved me from my dream," Thais objected. "She stopped me from choking myself."

I looked at her. "That's what she told you. Any chance she was doing the opposite? Tightening the twisted sheet around your neck, but then you woke up and stopped her?"

Thais frowned. "I don't know." She sighed and looked at the clock. It was almost 2 a.m. "So that still gives us Richard and Luc and those three. And Richard isn't just a really weird fifteen-year-old with tattoos and a pierced eyebrow. He's a grown-up. A really old grown-up in a kid's body."

I forced myself to say it. "What about Luc? He lied to us about so many things. Maybe he was trying to lull us into loving him so we wouldn't think he would try to kill us."

"I don't know," Thais said after a long pause. "I can't wrap my mind around it. Logically, it's possible. But I can't get myself there."

"Yeah. I know." I let my breath out, feeling incredibly tired. Well, finding out your entire life has been a web of lies can do that to a girl. "But still—we shouldn't be blind about this. He outright lied about so many things. Made us believe—I mean, he was way convincing, right? Who knows what he's capable of?" I said it, though something inside me just couldn't believe it. Then something else occurred to me.

"We're not out of danger," I said. "Especially with Nan still MIA. But I just thought of something—there's a spell."

I expected Thais to pull her sour-milk expression at the mention of a spell, and I wasn't disappointed. She was still finding it hard to get cozy with all the witch stuff, despite how much she'd loved the feel of magick at the Treize's circle.

"It's a spell where two people sort of share their power," I said, trying to remember where I'd seen it. "Like, people in love use it to strengthen their bond, make them closer. Or a parent might do it with a child to help with learning magick or make the child stronger. It makes it easier to join your powers together afterward. If we did it . . . both of us would be stronger—against anything that might come at us."

Thais nodded thoughtfully. "Is it dangerous?"

I frowned. "I don't think so. Let me get the book." I knew what she meant—Thais and I had done magick, shared a vision, and it had gotten weirdly huge and powerful, out of control, and I didn't know why. Our grandmo—Petra had told us that in our magickal *famille*, people were afraid of twins because their magick put together was frighteningly strong. I wasn't sure if that was true.

In the little house I shared with Nan, we had a living room, workroom, dining room, small bathroom, and kitchen on the first floor. Upstairs were two small bedrooms and another bathroom. Our workroom had bookcases full of magickal texts. The first time Thais had come into this house, she'd been horrified when she saw our books, our supplies for magick. I snickered now, thinking about it.

"Would it be indexed in the back?" Thais asked. "Can I help look?"

"Do you speak old French?"

"I don't even speak new French," she said. "Not much, anyway."

"Okay. Then just sit tight. I should be able to find it. . . ."

A few minutes later I had found it in an old *grimoire* that belonged to Nan. It was in Old French, which I wasn't completely fluent in but could hack my way through. The spell was called *"Joindre tous les deux,"* or "Join both."

Quickly I got our supplies together.

"Why do I feel like I'm in the Addams family?" Thais asked, watching me. "Aren't you leaving out the eye of newt, wing of bat?"

I looked at her. "You liked it at Axelle's house, the magick."

She lowered her eyes and quit smiling. "Yeah."

"Okay, get in," I said. Thais came to stand next to me as I drew a chalk circle around us on the workroom floor.

"You're really good at drawing circles," Thais said, sounding nervous.

"Lots of practice. Circle-drawing 101." I did it again with salt, then I got Nan's four pewter cups to represent the four elements and put them at the points of the compass. One held water, one held incense to represent air, one held dirt from our backyard to represent, well, earth, and one held a candle for fire.

"Fire is our element," I reminded Thais. "Every witch has an affinity with one element, and she focuses on that element in her magick. It makes it smoother, more effective."

I lit another candle and put it on the floor

between us. We sat cross-legged, facing each other. I found the right page again and began to read.

"Can you do it in English?" Thais asked.

I thought. "Well, it might be more effective in French—it all rhymes and everything. Sometimes the very words themselves hold magickal power."

"But I won't understand it," said Thais, and I thought I heard fear in her voice.

"And you think I'll turn you into a frog?"

Thais just looked unhappy.

"Okay, um, I think I can just translate this as I go," I muttered, reading down. "Maybe it doesn't really have to be in French. Let's see. First let's center ourselves and get in touch with our magick. Then I'll read this little section. There are four sections, and at each section, you'll combine two things together. I'll explain as we go. Okay?"

Thais nodded, looking uncertain.

I closed my eyes and reached out to barely touch the tips of my fingers to Thais's knees. After a moment, she did the same to me. "Slow your breathing," I said very softly. "Slow your mind. Let everything relax. Let go of fear and fatigue. Inside you is a joyous door that leads to magick. When you relax completely, the door doesn't open—it dissolves, letting you become one with magick. Magick is everywhere around you, in everything, living and inert. That's the strength and power we tap. Now breathe, very, very slowly."

From just the little connection I already had with Thais, I was in tune with her aura, and I could feel her gradually relax and become centered. It took several minutes, but as Nan said, quality magick takes time.

Slowly I opened my eyes and referred back to the book. My translation was clumsy, and it was hard to make it into a nice, smooth chant.

"I join with you, my sister, so that we will be one."

I had Thais repeat that, then I went on.

"We are of the same blood. Now let us be of the same heart and the same mind. I join with you and offer you my power and strength."

Thais repeated it.

"Water is our witness." I motioned to Thais, and she poured two silver cups of water into one larger cup.

"Air is our witness." Thais took two long incense sticks and held their tips together so that their thin spirals of smoke twined together like vines.

"Earth is our witness." Thais took white sand and black sand and rubbed them together in her palms, like salt and pepper. When they were evenly mixed, she dribbled them out of her hand into the rune shape I showed her, *goeffe*, which looks like an X. It stood for gift, partnership, generosity.

"Fire is our witness," I said. Thais picked up two smaller candles and lit them simultaneously from the candle between us. Then she set them into a small silver candleholder that had two joined stems.

"We join our strength and power," we said together, and I nodded at two small willow twigs. Thais tied them securely together in the middle with red string.

"Life is our witness."

I took a piece of chalk and drew the rune *quenne* on the floor. "This is for fire, our element," I said. "It's our passion, our creativity."

I gave Thais the piece of chalk and showed her the rune in the book that I wanted her to draw. She did. "*Lage* is for knowledge, creativity, psychic power," I said. "We call on the power of these runes to make our spell complete."

Then Thais and I put our hands on each other's shoulders and closed our eyes.

"*Nous voulons joindre nous tous les deux,*" I said. We said it together and then said it a third time. And that was when we got blown across the room.

I hit the wall headfirst and cried out. After several stunned moments, I slowly sat up, trying not to groan. Clio lay in a heap on the other side of the room, and I got up and ran to her. She was already blinking and trying to sit up.

"What the hell was that?" she said.

I knelt and put my arm around her. "Are you okay? You didn't say that would happen!"

Her eyes were wide, and she rubbed her head where it had hit a bookcase. "Because I didn't know!" she said. "We got blown right out of that circle! I've never heard of anything like that happening. Holy crap."

"Then what went wrong?" I asked.

"I have no fricking idea." Clio stood up and brushed off her butt. She rubbed her head again. "Ow. That has never, ever happened to me." She looked at me, and I felt the usual little spark of surprise that we looked so much alike. Her hair was longer, and our birthmarks were on opposite cheeks, but there was no doubt we were identical. "Maybe it was the twin-power thing," she said, sounding kind of awed.

"God. Well, no wonder everyone's freaked about

it." I realized I was shaking and looked over at the circle. The candles and incense had been snuffed out, and the salt circle wasn't even there anymore. "So are we joined now?"

We looked at each other, and I sent out a systems check to see if I felt different.

"I'm not sure," said Clio. "I don't know if the spell had time to work or what."

But as I stood there, I realized that I was picking up stuff from Clio—I could *feel* her next to me, but not physically. It was like I felt a form, a shape, next to me. Not like a ghost. Not even human-looking. But it was Clio, definitely Clio. I felt her puzzlement and excitement. I felt fear in myself, but not from her.

"Hey. Is that you?" I asked.

Looking amazed, Clio laughed and nodded. "I feel you too. It's like—Flubber. Like a Flubber Thais, only I can't see it. This is way cool."

"It's strange," I said. "I wonder if it works when we're farther apart."

"I guess we'll find out," she said, grinning.

At dawn I went back to Axelle's. I still didn't know how Axelle Gauvin had wrangled custody of me after Dad had died. A spell? Strings pulled? I hoped that Petra would come back soon and that I'd be able to live with her and Clio when she did.

In the meantime, all my stuff was in Axelle's apartment, in the French Quarter.

At dawn, in September, it was about eighty-five degrees. I walked down narrow, almost quiet streets, thinking how pretty the Quarter was with not many people in it. Later today it would be crowded and noisy and smell like beer and sunscreen.

I was still awed by the spell with Clio. I mean, I had gotten thrown eight feet across a room. By magick. It was hard to believe. Except I had a knot on my head to prove it. Clio said she would try to figure out what had gone wrong, but if she'd never even heard of anything like that happening . . .

I used my key and went through the wrought-iron side gate that led to Axelle's apartment. The narrow carriageway was cool and damp, and I could barely hear my shoes on the ancient flagstones, worn by centuries of use. The small courtyard was a mini-Eden, with birds fluttering around the subtropical plants that lined the tiny swimming pool.

And here was Axelle's front door. Despite feeling shaken by last night's spell, a new strength had solidified in me, and I felt complete and sure of myself. I opened the door and went in. As usual, the scent of cigarette smoke made my nostrils twitch. It was cool and dark inside, and as I shut the door, Minou, Axelle's cat, ran past my legs into the apartment.

"Thais."

My eyes were adjusting to the dim light, and I saw Axelle lying on her black leather couch. Putting aside the newspaper she was reading, she stood and came over to me.

"You're up early. Catching up on current events?" I said evenly, moving into the kitchen.

"Up all night. Reading the comics." Her dark

shiny pageboy swung right at her chin, every hair in place. She might have been awake for the previous twenty-four hours, but you'd never be able to tell. "So you stayed out all night. Another wasp attack?"

"More like shock and horror over my family's history." Not looking at her, I poured myself some orange juice and put two slices of bread into the toaster.

"Shock? Okay, I'll give you that. You had a lot dumped on you yesterday. But horror?" Her red lips formed a smile. She poured herself a glass of juice, then got a bottle of vodka from the top of the fridge. She splashed some into her orange juice and took an appreciative sip. It was barely 7 a.m.

"Thais," she said, with a warm, almost seductive note in her voice, "you've been handed the opportunity of a lifetime. The chance to become immortal—it's what fantasies are made of."

"Or nightmares," I said. "You guys, the ones I've met so far—the Treize—you're not exactly the poster kids for health and happiness."

Axelle stretched, her lithe, catlike body arching. "You might be surprised at how much pleasure one can experience with an endless lifetime to pursue it."

"News flash," I said. "Pleasure isn't the same thing as happiness." I felt bitter and angry that my life was entwined with the Treize at all. It wasn't that I hated Axelle—I didn't. But I didn't trust her, and we had nothing in common.

"Ooh," said Axelle, finishing her orange juice and vodka. "Such wisdom from one so *young*. But Thais, tell me you aren't happy to know you have a family, a background, a history. You know who you are and where you're from. Isn't that better than being a little boat adrift at sea?"

I didn't answer as I ate my toast. She had me. My whole life, it had been just me and my dad. When he'd died, I'd had no one—just a family friend, a neighbor who cared about me. But no family. It was true—I'd felt lost. Then Axelle had brought me to New Orleans, and Clio and I had found each other. Discovering that I had a sister and a grandmother was like winning the lottery. I belonged to someone. I wasn't alone.

Then I'd found out they were witches. I'd never taken witchcraft or Wicca or any of that stuff seriously—I'd thought it was all a joke. The disappointment that they were involved in it had been sharp and immediate. Now . . . I was more used to the idea. I accepted that it ran in *my* blood too. But it hadn't been what I wanted. And after last night's explosive spell, my doubts seemed justified.

I'd found my family, and they were witches.

I'd found my soul mate, my true love, and he had betrayed me.

And all of this was woven into the unbelievable, movie-plot background that Petra, Axelle, Luc, and a bunch of other people were in fact still experiencing a spell that had been set into motion in 1763, more than 240 years ago. They were immortal.

Now they wanted to make me and Clio immortal too. And we had to decide.

I felt Axelle's eyes on me and hoped my feelings

weren't transparent. Immortality. Luc was immortal—he would never age. If we had stayed together, I would get old and die someday, and he wouldn't, ever. But if I were immortal . . .

It wouldn't even matter, because we wouldn't be together, because he was a lying, cheating bastard.

I heard footsteps on the wooden stairs that led to Axelle's attic workroom. Great. Now I had to deal with Daedalus or Jules, who practically lived here.

"Is she back yet?"

The voice came to me in the kitchen and sent chills down my spine.

"Can't you call Petra?" Luc went on, crossing the dimly lit room.

Axelle waited till he was in sight, then wordlessly pointed to me, a small cat's smile on her face.

Luc stopped short when he saw me.

I glanced at him for a second, just long enough to stop my heart and sear his image into my brain. Luc. Unlike Axelle, he did look like he'd been up all night. He was in the same clothes as yesterday. His face was darkened by a day's worth of beard. His eyes, the color of the sky at twilight, were upset, shadowed.

Good.

"Thais." He took a step closer and I saw him run a hand through his disheveled, too-long dark hair. I turned and put my plate in the sink, unable to swallow.

"I was worried," he said, and it sounded like getting those words out cost him. I was all too aware of Axelle's black, interested eyes following this exchange like a tennis match.

I tried to wipe any expression from my face and turned back to him.

"And this matters because . . . ?" I said coolly.

He frowned. "Are you okay, then?"

"I'm fine. I mean, my heart hasn't been ripped out and stomped on *today*." I was surprising myself—it was like I could channel my inner bitch all of a sudden. I'd never spoken so coldly to anyone in my life.

Luc flushed, which of course increased his gorgeousness level to about a forty-seven on a scale from one to ten. "That isn't fair," he said in a low voice, and I saw his hands clench at his sides.

"Unfair? *You're* talking to *me* about unfair?" I felt my cheeks heat with anger. "Are you *nuts?* Who the hell do you think you are?"

Suddenly I felt like I was going to lose it in a huge, humiliating way. I spun and stalked to my room, which was a little addition past the kitchen. I slammed the door behind me, but it hit Luc's shoulder with a thud and he shoved it open so hard it crashed against the wall, rattling the pictures.

I'd never seen him look so angry, not even on that horrible night when Clio and I had found out he'd been two-timing us—with each other. I still felt sick when I thought of it.

"I think I'm *yours*," he said furiously. I backed away from him until I reached my bed, but I wasn't scared. I was furious too, my anger and pain rising in me like a tidal wave.

"I think I was made for you and you for me," he

went on, his jaw clenched and his body rigid with tension. "I think I found you just when I wanted to die. I think I found someone to live for. At last."

I was in hell. This was what hell was.

"But I screwed up," he said. "I made a huge mistake because I was stupid and scared—" He stopped suddenly, as if startled that word had left his lips. "I screwed up," he said more calmly. "I'm sorrier than I can say. I regret it more than anything." He looked into my eyes, and he was so familiar to me, so much who I loved, that I wanted to scream. "Out of 260 years' worth of regrets, this is the biggest one."

I couldn't breathe. My heart was pounding so hard it was a physical pain in my chest. Here's the really humiliating part: *I wanted to buy it,* to say, I forgive you. I wanted to reach out and grab him and hold his head in my hands so I could kiss him hard, *hard.* I wanted to pull him down onto my bed with me and feel him pressed all against me, like I had before, on the levee by the river. I wanted it so much I could taste it, feel it.

"Thais," he said, moving closer, his voice much softer. "Hit me if you want. Throw things at me. Yell and scream and curse my name until your voice is gone. But come back to me. I'll spend the rest of my life trying to make it up to you." He paused. "Which is saying something." The rest of his life would be quite a long time. Unless he used the Treize's spell to die.

Still I couldn't speak. My eyes felt wide and huge, staring at him with a longing so deep it felt like thirst.

He reached out one hand and slowly, slowly

stroked one finger up my bare arm. His hands, his knowing hands, had been all over my body, and the memory of it choked me.

My brain was shorting out. My world was telescoping inward till it contained only me and Luc. I swallowed hard.

"No," I said, in a barely audible whisper. I pulled my arm away from his touch and drew in a shuddering breath. "No."

He took a step back, searching my face. I saw new pain in his eyes, as if I could see hope actually dying, and I looked away.

"I could make you love me," he said, his voice low and tense again.

Cold reason dumped into my brain. I met his eyes again.

"You think? Like with a *spell?*"

His jaw tightened. Then he looked down, and I saw both shame and despair on his face. "Thais, I—" He started to raise a hand, then dropped it. He looked at me for a long time, then finally turned and left my room. As soon as he was through the door, I shut it behind him and locked it.

Then I sat on my bed, shaking, and waited for the tears to come.

St. Louis Cemetery No. 1

The tombstones were speckled with lichen and moss, the result of hundreds of years of heat and humidity. Ouida thought they looked beautiful, and she focused her camera at a barely readable inscription. With the grainy black-and-white film she was using, this image would be striking, melancholy, like the cemetery itself. She checked the light meter and decided to underexpose the film so that the inscription would show up darker. Angling her camera on its tripod, she carefully clicked the shutter, then stood back, pleased. That would come out well.

Cemeteries fascinated her. Maybe it was like looking through the window of an exclusive club to which she'd never belong. A quiet laugh escaped her, and she covered her mouth, not wanting to be overheard.

Once her tripod was stowed, Ouida looked around, feeling a light gray sense of—not dread, it wasn't that bad; maybe just sadness?—descend on her. There was another reason she was in St. Louis Cemetery No. 1 besides just a photo op.

Head down, she started walking to the far southeast corner, one of the first areas to have been filled in, back in the 1790s. God, that had been a long time ago. Yet the memories of it were still sharply engraved in her mind, not softened or weathered by time.

A few minutes' walking brought her to a place she visited every time she was in New Orleans. There was a small bench opposite the family crypt, and she sat on it, putting down her camera equipment bag. The sun was hot, reflecting off the white marble everywhere, the cement-sealed tombs. People had learned long ago to clear a graveyard of trees unless they wanted thick roots to start popping coffins out of the ground ten years down the road.

Ouida thought of all the winters she'd spent freezing up in Massachusetts. She was a southerner, all right. The cold had gone right through her bones to her marrow. Here the heat seemed to melt through her skin, softening her inside, relaxing layers of tension. She was more at home here, more herself. But the burden of memories was so much easier to bear in Massachusetts. She knew she'd return.

After several minutes, Ouida frowned. Someone was coming. Someone she knew. She let her mind expand into the space around her, let slim tendrils of awareness pick up information in a growing circle.

Daedalus.

A minute later he appeared, looking incongruous in a black polo shirt and tan linen pants.

"Ouida," he said. "I thought I felt you over here."

He regarded her, then looked around. Seeing the name on the tomb opposite her, he smiled thinly. "'La Famille Martin,'" he read. "'Armand. Gregoire. Antonine.' Still rehashing the past, eh, Ouida?"

It was not something she was going to discuss with him. "What are you doing here?"

He shrugged and, uninvited, sat next to her on the bench. "Collecting useful things." He gestured to the canvas shopping bag he held. "There are always broken graves in a cemetery this old. Sometimes one can find the occasional bone for one's supply cabinet. Also, Spanish moss, other mosses, any number of useful things."

Ouida looked at him with distaste, and he laughed. "What, you get your bones from a mail-order catalog? Please."

"I don't seem to do many spells that call for human bones, Daedalus."

"Don't give me that superior attitude, Ouida," he said, not angrily. "We've always known that our interests are different." He waved a hand around the cemetery. "Plus, you know, I always check for Melita."

Ouida was truly surprised. "Check for her? As if she might be buried somewhere? You're kidding. How could she possibly be dead?"

Daedalus shrugged. "Most likely she isn't. But I've come to believe there's a slim chance the rite may have affected her differently somehow—maybe because of all the magick she'd done before or for some other reason. After all, it killed Cerise. So maybe it did something different to Melita. There's always hope, however far-fetched. The important thing would be to find her, dead or alive, before she found any of us."

Ouida scoffed. "She's had two hundred years to find us if she wanted. None of us has been in hiding."

"Yes, but now we're trying to do the rite," Daedalus reminded her.

"Or at least you are," Ouida returned.

Daedalus frowned. "We all are. Everyone is."

Ouida didn't say anything. Gathering bones? Looking for Melita? What was Daedalus actually doing here? Did he know something about Melita that he hadn't told anyone? Had he found her? Could he even be in league with her or somehow have usurped her power?

Ouida shook her head, aware that Daedalus was watching her. She'd blocked her thoughts and knew he couldn't be eavesdropping. She had her secrets, just as Daedalus did. She sighed. The Treize was about as safe and trustworthy as an adder's nest.

Red with Her Blood

Rocks. If there was one thing Louisiana had over Ireland, it was that there were no cursed rocks in the ground. Plowing was easy there. The dirt was rich and black, bursting with life and nourished by the Delta basin.

Here the soil was thin and pale gray, and you couldn't spit without hitting rock after rock after rock. Marcel had been working this same plot of ground for, what, seven years now? Yet each spring and each autumn, he managed to plow up yet another ton of rocks, as if the earth herself were slowly pushing them to the surface all throughout the year.

And maybe she was.

Marcel paused and wiped his wet brow with the coarse brown wool of his monk's robe, then bent his back over the hand-powered plow again. Earth. Giver of life. Mindlessly he watched as the thick steel blade cut through the thin turf and peeled it up in two curling layers. He heard the chink of the blade hitting a rock, of course, because he'd gone about four inches, and he knelt to wrest it up and add it to the growing pile by the side of the field. It would become part of a wall, like the rest.

The ground was cold as his fingers scrabbled around the large stone. It was September; soon it would be winter here and bitter, with icy winds borne off the western sea. Marcel's fingers grabbed the rock, and suddenly he felt something slice his finger.

Wincing, he pulled up his hand and found an ancient shard of glass embedded in his skin. Good job. Carefully he pulled the shard out and was surprised by the sudden rush of blood from the relatively small cut. In seconds the blood had run across his hand and begun dripping onto the ground. He'd better get to the infirmary, have Brother Niall do something.

He glanced down, and with no warning, Marcel was hurled back through time, to another place, another life.

It had been dark, pouring rain, but with every flash of lightning Marcel had seen how the wet ground beneath Cerise was red with her blood. He closed his eyes, blinking hard, not wanting to remember.

He'd fallen in love with her. He'd been seventeen. She'd been fourteen but already a woman, doing a woman's work. She'd laughed and spurned him, saying that she was too young to settle down, that she was content to stay at home with her mother and sister.

He'd courted her for years, leaving flowers on her doorstep, freshly killed rabbits outside her kitchen. She had been easy to love, her face bright and open, that golden hair like sunlight spun into silk. Her eyes had been as green as Irish hills in springtime, and she'd had a small red mark on her cheek, like a crushed flower.

It had been just Cerise, her mother, and her sister at home. Petra's husband, Armand, had run off to New Orleans years before. Marcel could barely remember him. He'd been tall, with black hair. But Marcel couldn't picture his face.

The Martins had needed a man about the house; that much was clear. Marcel had taken it upon himself to chop wood for them, to bring their cow in from the woods. Melita, the older sister, had been as dark as their father and dark in other ways as well. Almost every man in the village had watched her, wanted her. But not Marcel. Cerise's sunlight was infinitely preferable to Melita's darkness.

For years Marcel dedicated himself to Cerise and her family, hoping that she would relent, take him for her husband, that she would be his. After everything he had done, how could she do else? But she'd made him no promises and laughed lightly whenever he'd brought it up.

She hadn't been unkind or cruel. But it was like trying to catch a fairy made of light and air—impossible to pin down. Of course, he'd been going about it all wrong. He'd come to realize that.

Now, kneeling on the cold Irish ground, Marcel swallowed hard and shut his eyes against the relentless memories—once started, they were unstoppable. He'd been walking through the woods to check his traps and had heard Cerise's laughter. From a distance he had spied her, running among the trees, the dappled sunlight occasionally catching her bright hair. Marcel had smiled to see Cerise, a girl of seventeen, still playing tag.

Even when he'd seen who was chasing her, he'd still thought it was a game. Richard Landry was barely fifteen, though he'd become tall in the last year. Still a boy, compared to Marcel's twenty years. Marcel had started walking toward them, already knowing what he would say, how he'd tease them for playing like children.

But then he'd seen Richard catch Cerise, heard her startled gasp of laughter. He'd seen Richard hold Cerise's wrists above her head and press her against the broad trunk of a sycamore. When had the boy gotten taller than she? Marcel was still, like a deer, watching them between the thick trees. He waited for Cerise to push Richard away, perhaps angrily, to chastise him for taking liberties. Not even Marcel had held her so close.

But Richard had dared more. He'd leaned against her, lowered his head to kiss her. For a few moments Cerise ducked away, still laughing breathlessly, but then she had stilled, and Richard's mouth had taken hers. He'd let go of her hands and she'd held his shoulders, her eyes wide at first with astonishment, then drifting closed with pleasure.

Marcel had gaped, speechless. He himself had never kissed Cerise! He'd tried several times, but she'd evaded him and he hadn't pushed her. Now he saw his approach had been too mild-mannered.

Richard's wasn't, by any means. He'd wedged his knee between her legs, through her long cotton skirts. They'd been touching from chin to ankle, Richard's hands braced on the tree behind her.

Marcel didn't know how long he'd stood there, feeling lightning-struck. After an endless while, Richard and Cerise had separated, staring at each other. Richard had been breathing hard, his face dark with intent. He moved toward her again, but this time Cerise pushed him away. She'd picked up her skirts and run through the woods, back to the village.

After that, Marcel had begun to pursue Cerise with more purpose and less patience. Again and again she'd said no to him, giving him one excuse after another. She'd continued to laugh at him and evade him. Until that one time, down by the river.

He could still smell the water, feel the heaviness of the air. The heat had made them light-headed. Cerise's eyes had looked up into his. And he had tasted heaven.

Then Marcel was in another memory. He was running through the dark woods, woods he knew like his own home. Spanish moss brushed against his face as he tracked Melita. That night he'd seen her work her evil magick, seen her split the huge oak in two, destroying the Source that bubbled from beneath its roots. The tree had fallen and burned.

And Marcel had followed her. Cerise was dead, and it was Melita's fault. Melita had wanted only power at any price, even the cost of her sister's life. She'd worked her rite, maybe even knowing it would kill Cerise—or at least not caring when it had. Marcel had seen Melita's face that night at the circle, her beautiful face, laughing, drunk with magick, flushed with ecstasy—while her younger sister died giving birth to her bastard daughter.

Cerise should have married him. He'd begged her to. He feared he knew the reason she wouldn't.

Now she was dead, her sunlight entombed forever. Marcel would never see or kiss or hold her again. As long as he lived, he would never love another. So Marcel had followed Melita that night, through the darkness. And he'd caught up with her.

Early on Thursday, I went to Axelle's to get Thais. I'd been thinking, and I wanted us to do another spell—hopefully one that wouldn't go nuclear on us. In one of Nan's books, I'd found a spell that could reveal other spells. Maybe it would help us figure out who was behind the attacks on us.

Parking in the French Quarter was a fantasy, so I'd called Thais and asked her to wait outside for me. When I drove down Axelle's block at like two miles an hour behind a tourist-laden horse carriage, I saw her standing by the curb.

"Hey," she said, sliding into my little blue Camry. "No school. Yay."

"We love teacher workdays," I said.

"Yes, we do," said Thais. "A three-school-day week seems about right. So did you do it? Last night?"

For a second I didn't know what she was talking about, but then I remembered that last night had been when I was supposed to open the cupboard where Nan had left emergency instructions.

"Yeah," I said. "I couldn't open it. She told me

exactly what to do, and I think I did it right, but no dice."

Thais turned to me, her eyes worried. I made a bunch of left turns until we were headed uptown again.

"So what now?" she asked. "You don't know where she is or how to get in touch with her."

Thais sounded slightly disapproving: that reckless Nan, leaving me on my own.

"I'll give her one more day," I said. "Then I'm going to ask Ouida for help."

"Okay, good idea," Thais agreed. "Where are we going?"

"To Racey's. I didn't feel that safe at home," I admitted. I drove across the eight lanes of Canal Street and started heading up St. Charles Avenue. A streetcar rattled past us, and I waited till its noise had passed to ask, "How are things at Axelle's?"

Thais rubbed her forehead. "Tense. Daedalus and Jules were over last night. And Richard popped in to say hello. He still weirds me out."

"Were they trying to get you to do the rite? Did you feel safe there?"

"Yes, and not really. I mean, I know all these people, but not that well. I just feel so nervous all the time around everyone, like any minute some crazy thing is going to jump out and start attacking me. Plus Richard totally creeps me out just because. I mean, he looks younger than us, but then I remember he's like 260 years old. He's a grown-up."

It was definitely weird—kind of mind-blowing

that any of the Treize were immortal, but especially the ones who looked so young still, like Richard and the girl, Manon.

And of course there was the other member of their little group who'd been frozen forever at his age, looking so fricking gorgeous . . .

"Anyone else drop by?" I asked casually, my eyes on the road.

"No," said Thais. "I was hoping Ouida would, but I guess she's busy. Axelle said most of them are trying to rent apartments in case they're here for a while."

"Makes sense. Did you tell anyone about the kablooey magick?"

"No. Were you able to figure out what went wrong?"

"Nope. I went over everything I could think of. All I can come up with is it's the combination of you and me."

"And now you want to do it again?" Thais sounded less than enthusiastic.

"A different spell. And in a different place and with Racey. That should fix it."

A few minutes later I turned off St. Charles toward the lake and turned again on Willow Street. Racey's family had a medium-size house built over a full basement. Basements sat on top of the ground here—you couldn't dig cellars for the same reason you couldn't bury people underground. The water table was too high.

As usual, there were three or four cats hanging around outside the house, and Chelsea, one of

Racey's dogs, made a show of alertness at the top of the stairs, fierce guard dog on duty, before letting her head sink onto her paws again and closing her eyes.

I knocked hard on the screen door because their doorbell had been broken as long as I could remember. Ceci, one of Racey's older sisters, opened the door. She was holding a bagel in one hand—it was pretty early.

"Yo," she said, then saw Thais standing next to me. She blinked, looked from me to Thais and back again. Then she grinned and shook some of her dark, purple-streaked hair off her shoulders. "Racey told me about the Doublemint action," she said. "Whew. When you go identical, you really go identical." She let us into the house, then turned her head and yelled, "Hey, guys! Come check this out!"

I glanced at Thais, who seemed a little timid and bemused. *Not so identical,* I thought.

Bill and Hillary, Racey's other two dogs, trotted into the room. They sniffed me—same Clio—and then with interest sniffed Thais, the different Clio.

"Hey, puppy," Thais said, holding her hand out to them. "What kind of dogs are these?"

"Catahoula hounds," I said, leading the way to the kitchen. Racey's house was at least twice as big as mine, with six rooms downstairs and four bedrooms on the second floor. We went through the foyer and the dining room, then into the big kitchen/family room. Azura, Racey's mom, was at her sewing machine, surrounded by a big puddle of purple fabric.

"Hi, Clio," she said, looking up with a smile; then she saw Thais. She took the pins out of her mouth and stood up to come over to us. I felt Thais's self-consciousness.

"Azura, this is my sister, Thais," I said. "This is Racey's mom, Azura Copeland."

"Welcome, my dear," said Racey's mom, and gave Thais a hug.

Thais was smiling when they separated, and then I heard footsteps running down the stairs. "Mom! Make Trey get out of the bathroom!" Racey said, stomping into the kitchen. Trey was Racey's brother, a year younger than us. He went to our school, and he and Racey were always yelling at each other about something. "Hey, guys. I'm almost ready." She turned back to Azura. "I mean, we have two other bathrooms. Does he have to hog the one that has my makeup in it?"

"I doubt you need makeup on for what you're going to do," Racey's mom said dryly. "Go do your thing, and I'll get Trey out of the bathroom."

Racey scowled. "Whatever." Nodding at us, she said, "Come on. We might as well go."

She opened the back door and headed down the wooden steps that led to their backyard.

"Our workroom is back here," Racey tossed over her shoulder, for Thais's benefit. "It used to be a garden shed, I guess."

Racey's backyard, like so many yards in New Orleans, was basically an overgrown jungle. There was a thicket of banana trees along one side fence and another clump of enormous ginger plants overhanging the shed. Some of Azura's favorite bamboo was threatening to take over the yard, and I wondered if Thais would recognize the happy, healthy grove of marijuana plants in the back of the tiny vegetable garden. Racey's dad grew them for people with cancer who were going through chemo.

Racey's dad was an artist, and he'd painted a huge sun on the door of the shed. Inside, two small windows and a cracked skylight illuminated the walls and floor, all of which were covered with symbols, runes, and magickal words.

Of course, I'd seen all this a million times, but I wondered what Thais was making of it. She stopped on the threshold and looked around. I guessed they didn't have anything like this in Welsford, Connecticut, where she'd grown up. Racey went to their cabinet and started getting out supplies. I opened Nan's book and started flipping through the pages to find the right spell.

"What's this?" Thais said, tracing her fingers over a symbol.

I looked up. "Uh, *sain et sauf*," I said. "Like, safe and sound. Safety. For protection."

"Like those runes from the other night?"

"No—those were runes. *Sain et sauf* is a magickal symbol but not from any runic alphabet."

"There's more than one rune alphabet?"

"Several," said Racey, setting out her family's four cups. Theirs were made of green marble.

"But our branch of the, uh"—I translated in my

head—"natural religion has symbols of its own that are centuries old and very powerful."

"Is the natural religion the *Bonne Magie* you were telling me about?"

"Yeah," I said absently, trailing my finger down the page. "You have any tiger's eyes?" I asked Racey.

"I'll look. What else? Copper?"

"No. Gold. And give me four stones of protection, whatever you've got."

"Okay, let's see," Racey murmured, rooting around in the cabinet. "I've got, well, here's another tiger's eye. I've got some agate and malachite. Jet. Citrine?"

I mentally reviewed their properties. "That should be good. Skip the second tiger's eye. Don't want to be unbalanced." I turned back to Thais while Racey started drawing a circle on the floor. "*Magie Naturelle* is like the big, general, French-based form of Wicca, in a way. Like there's Wicca, and then there are different types of Wicca."

Thais frowned. "There are?"

Oh, *déesse,* she had so much to learn. I was glad I wasn't in her shoes. "Yeah, Like Pictish, Scottish, and so on. A bunch. For us, the natural religion is the umbrella religion. Our own *famille's* branch of it we call *Bonne Magie.*"

"I've heard Petra call it *Chose Nous,*" added Racey. "'Our thing.'"

"Like the Mafia?" Thais asked faintly. "*Cosa Nostra?*"

Maybe we were giving her too much info for the

moment. "Yeah," I said. "Exactly like that. Except we're French witches drawing on the eternal mystical energy in everything around us to work good, and they're Italian and they kill people. Other than that, just like."

Thais looked a little embarrassed.

I drew her into the circle and Racey closed it behind us. We sat cross-legged on the floor, facing each other.

"Okay, so what are we doing now?" Racey asked.

I realized I hadn't gotten her caught up on the soap opera in, like, days. I let out a deep breath, wondering where to start.

"Someone's trying to hurt me and Clio," said Thais. "To kill us."

Racey looked from Thais to me. "Huh?"

"Things have gotten weird," I said, in a massive understatement.

"You mean, weirder than having a surprise identical twin and then God's gift dating both of you at once?" Racey said bluntly.

"Yes. Weirder than that," I said, suddenly feeling tired. "Nan hasn't come back yet. And as it turns out, God's gift actually belongs to a coven that Nan used to belong to. He's a witch."

"Wow." Racey whistled. "Good riddance."

"Yes," I said, my throat feeling tight. "On top of all this, the fun just keeps coming. Both Thais and I have had, like, near-death experiences." I filled Racey in on Thais's nightmare with the snake, the almost stabbing that Racey had witnessed, the streetcar accident, the wasps.

"So we want to do a spell to show us who's behind

all this," I went on. "I mean, I'm not thrilled staying in that house alone, and Thais is still living with Axelle, and Nan's not back yet."

"You should both come stay here," Racey said, frowning. "Jeez. Why didn't you come here last night?"

"I stayed up late, trying to work Nan's cupboard spell, and then it was too late," I said.

Racey smacked my knee. "Frickin' idiot. It's never too late, you know that. Tell me you're coming here tonight."

"I might," I said. "If nothing's better by then. In the meantime, let's see if this thing works."

The three of us formed a triangle, sitting inside the circle. I picked up the four stones of protection. "One stone for us, one stone for the problem, one stone for the past, and one stone for the future," I said, putting them in a square around us.

"Do you have an element?" Thais asked Racey.

"Yeah, of course," Racey said, surprised. She tugged on the chain of her necklace and showed Thais the large moonstone pendant she wore. "Earth. I use a crystal to represent it. Also, you know, it's pretty and sets off my tan."

I lit the candle in the center for me and Thais.

Then we all held hands, and I read the spell, translating for Thais's benefit. It was much prettier in French, and I always like it when things rhyme. But oh, well.

> We walk in sunlight
> Shadows follow us.

We are facing fire
We are standing beneath stone
We are underwater
A storm is coming toward us.
With these words reveal the signature
Give the shadow a face, a name.
Show us who kindles fire against us
Who holds a stone over us
Who pulls us underwater
Who conjures a storm to destroy us.

Then I focused on the candle and started to sing my own personal power song, which sort of had words and sort of didn't. Its sounds had their basis in ancient words, but though the power was still there, the words themselves had leached away, leaving pure sound, pure magick.

After a minute, Racey started twining her song in and around mine, under and over and through. We looked up at each other and smiled. We'd done this too many times to count, yet each time it was fresh and new and exciting.

I didn't expect Thais to say anything—there was no way for her to know her personal song yet. It was something that developed over a period of years as you studied magick. But then a third voice joined in. I looked at Thais in surprise and saw that she was singing softly, watching the candle. I didn't recognize the form of her song, but it sounded real, not like gibberish. Racey and I exchanged glances, and then we all looked at the candle and sang.

Two voices singing are balanced, one against the other, and they can make a pure and beautiful magick. But somehow Thais's voice centered us, the way a three-legged stool is more stable than a two-legged ladder. And while Thais's speaking voice was incredibly similar to mine, our singing voices were different. Hers was more ethereal somehow. To my ears, mine sounded sharper and stronger, and hers was smoother and more flowy.

This was pretty much the most ambitious spell I'd ever tried without a teacher, and I had no idea what to expect. Our three voices raised and fell and joined and separated, and Thais's voice became stronger and more sure. I felt the magick rising in and around us, felt our combined energy swell. It was really beautiful, and happiness rose in me.

And that was when we got blown across the room.

What's Going On

Petra saw Richard even before she parked the car. He was leaning against the iron gate, looking up at her house. Were his lips moving? She couldn't tell. With a deep, exhausted sigh she got out of her car, then pulled her suitcase out of the back. If he felt her coming, he didn't show it.

"Hello, Riche," she said, and he turned to look at her.

"Honey, you're home," he said. "At last. You've missed some excitement."

Her gaze sharpened as she opened the gate, muttering a nulling spell so Richard could follow her in. That is, if Clio had kept up the layers of protection. "What kind of excitement?" she asked, starting up the steps.

Richard took the suitcase out of her hand and carried it up for her. He was wiry but surprisingly strong, Petra knew.

Inside the house Petra cast her senses but didn't feel Clio. She turned to face Richard. "What kind of excitement?" she asked again. "Where's Clio?"

He shrugged. "If she's not here, I don't know.

Nothing's happened to her that I've heard of. I mean, except the Treize."

"What about the Treize?" Petra said, feeling her nerves quicken.

"How about some tea?" Richard said. "Iced, if you have it. And for God's sake, turn on the air."

Petra stepped closer to him and looked up into his brown eyes, the color of coffee with a tiny bit of milk. "Tell me what I want to know and cut the crap," she said quietly.

He laughed. "Or you'll what, turn me into a frog?" He shook his head. "As far as I know, both girls are fine. But while you were gone, they confronted Axelle, and she called a meeting, and everyone showed, except for monk boy and slut girl, and they basically told the twins everything."

Petra felt a weight settle on her chest. She turned from Richard and walked back to the kitchen, where she opened the window and the back door and turned on the ceiling fan. The kitchen was messy, with unwashed dishes and glasses on the counters, the trash bag overfull, a rotten banana playing host to a happy horde of fruit flies. Yet Petra could detect the faint signature of Clio's presence, feel her vibrations lingering in the air. She had been here recently, like this morning. She was a slob, but alive.

Richard sat in one of the kitchen chairs, and Q-Tip ran into the room. Petra saw that his dish had food in it and his water was full. She stooped to pet him, trying to gather her thoughts.

Damn it. Her errand had taken longer than she'd

thought, but she'd still hoped that the Treize hadn't moved on the twins yet. She'd wanted to be the one who told them. Well, too late now. She stood and poured iced tea for herself and Richard, then sat down opposite him.

"Okay," she said. "Tell me what's going on."

He drank his tea, then shrugged. "Just what I told you. The Treize—"

"You included?"

"Hell, yeah. You think I'd miss that freak show? Yeah, so the Treize gathered and they dumped our sordid past in the twins' pretty laps, and then we had a circle."

Petra tried to hide the dismayed look in her eyes, with no success.

"A circle?"

Richard nodded and drank more tea. Q-Tip jumped up on his lap, and Richard petted him. "Yeah. It was very exciting. Your Thais—*elle a mordu admirablement au magie*. Like a duck to water."

Petra felt Richard's eyes on her. She loved Richard—she'd always loved him. It had pained her when he'd so obviously wanted Cerise. Cerise had rebuffed him, laughed and called him a little boy. Petra had seen Richard's hurt and been sorry for it. And Marcel had looked daggers at him.

Then Cerise had died. Marcel had broken down, had been so publicly full of grief. But Richard had kept it all inside. He'd overlain his boyish demeanor with a grown-up's cynicism and coldness.

Now, looking at him, his handsome adolescent face that would never achieve its full beauty in adulthood, she felt pangs of sorrow again, for the first time in years. Having the twins know about her past, having the Treize gathering again . . . It was all bringing up so many memories—memories that she'd hoped would stay buried.

"I'm sorry—" she began, then stopped, startled by the admission.

Richard raised one sardonic eyebrow at her.

Petra swallowed. "I'm sorry Cerise turned you down," she said. "You would have been a good match in a few years. I preferred you to Marcel. But he had done so much—"

She'd never before addressed him so directly about Cerise. Everything they'd both felt had been kept to themselves all this time. Why rub salt in the wound? And now, looking at the ice that crackled in Richard's eyes, she wished she'd kept silent.

Q-Tip jumped down and ran out the back door, as if the room's tension were too much for him. Petra leaned her head on her hand, looking down at the wooden grain of the kitchen table.

After a long pause, Richard shifted in his chair. "The Treize told Thais and Clio about the Source, the rite, Melita. They'll have a lot of questions for you, I imagine." His voice sounded distant, impersonal. "Also, it appears that Luc's own personal brand of magick is still going strong."

"What?"

Richard shrugged. "It came out that both girls are incredibly pissed at him, and the tension between the three of them would stop a train."

"Damn it," said Petra. "That fast? Both of them? I'll have to have a talk with Luc, then." Her lips thinned as she thought about how that conversation would go. She let out her breath, wishing she could lie down and sleep for a year. "I'd hoped for more time," she said. "It's all starting much too soon, too fast. Everything I've been dreading for so long."

"So you dread it then, do you?" Richard asked.

Petra looked up quickly. Richard had been hanging out with Daedalus and Jules, presumably to help them, for whatever reason. It was very possible he was here today to get an idea of exactly where Petra stood.

She spoke carefully. "Richard—I've been protecting the twins for seventeen years. Whatever Daedalus thinks might happen with the rite, whatever the rest of us could do with it or would want it for—we're still not sure. No one can be positive about its effects. Whether doing it is inevitable or not, yes, there are times when I absolutely dread finding out."

He nodded calmly, looking at her, then finished his tea and stood up. "I hear you. I think it's half-baked myself. But it's fun to watch the old boy run around."

Petra followed him to the front door. He opened it and stepped through, then turned to look back at her.

"Cerise didn't turn me down," he said quietly. Then he was down the front steps and gone before Petra could find her voice.

I lay on the floor next to the cabinet. The left side of my face felt like it had gotten hit with a baseball bat. Trying not to groan, I eased myself to a sitting position. It had happened *again*. I felt horrible—shaky and scared, like I'd been zapped by lightning or stuck my finger in a light socket. Gingerly I touched my cheek and pain shot into my skull. I'd hit myself even harder this time, since the garden shed/workroom was smaller than Clio's workroom. Less room for me to get thrown.

"Are you guys okay?" I asked, looking over at them.

Racey was lying on her back in the corner, muttering curses.

"Holy mother!" Clio said. "What is happening to us?"

Just then the shed door was flung open and Mrs. Copeland was there, her eyes wide.

"What happened?" she cried, hurrying to Racey. "What are y'all doing out here?"

Racey's sister Ceci rushed in next. After a quick

glance around, she said, "Race, what did I tell you about conjuring demons?"

"Very funny," Clio muttered, rubbing her shoulder.

"What were you doing?" Mrs. Copeland said again, her arm around Racey. Her long black braid swung over one shoulder. She looked barely older than her daughters.

Racey shook her head, wincing. "Just a normal spell."

"A *rélever la griffe*," Clio explained.

Mrs. Copeland frowned. "To see other spells? And what happened?"

"I don't know," Clio said slowly, looking at me. Instinctively I felt that she didn't want me to mention the twin-magick thing. "I was following the form, right from Nan's book. We were singing, just normal stuff, stuff we've done before, and then kablooey."

I felt Mrs. Copeland looking at me.

"Are you trained in magick?" she asked gently.

My face burned. Was this all my fault because I didn't know what I was doing? She left Racey and came over to turn my face carefully to the light. "You need ice on this," she said, looking concerned. "All of you need arnica. Ceci, go put the kettle on. I'll make some tea."

Standing up, she looked around the room, at the circle that had all but disappeared. "What was this?" she asked, pointing to a small black pile of gray dust.

"Uh, jet," Clio said. "I'll get you a new one. Sorry."

"It doesn't matter, sweetie. But you guys, do not repeat that spell unless Petra can be with you, okay?"

"Don't worry," I muttered. Right then I never wanted to do magick again.

We were all so upset that after Mrs. Copeland patched us up, we were forced to go to Botanika and have cheesecake and iced mocha frappés.

"It's either this or go buy shoes," Clio said, stirring her drink glumly.

Racey nodded. "I have to say, that totally sucked. But at least I don't have a shiner."

I made a face. Though Racey's mom had given me stuff to help with the pain and swelling, I still had a black eye. She'd given me arnica to take home with me and said it would help clear it up really fast, but still, I had a sort of bar-fight look going on that I hated.

"This has to be my fault," I said, stirring my drink. "This never happened to either of you before I came along. I think . . . maybe my magick is just off somehow. Or it just doesn't work right."

"That's a possibility," Racey said thoughtfully. "Tell me, are you a spawn of Satan? That would explain it."

I looked at her in horror, and Racey said, "Ouch!" when Clio kicked her under the table.

"Don't tease her," Clio said, then turned to me. "Our religion doesn't even believe in Satan or the devil or anything like that. There's nothing wrong with you. I don't know what's going on, but I'm sure there's an explanation. If only Nan—"

I nodded. If only Petra would come home.

The brass bells tied to Botanika's door jingled, and I saw my friend Sylvie Allen come in. She was the first person who'd been nice to me when I started school here, and we were in the same homeroom and several classes together. She was with her boyfriend and another guy.

"Hey!" I said, waving, happy to see her. She was so normal. Not a witch. Not immortal. It was a relief.

"Thais!" Sylvie came over, concern on her face. "Are you okay? What happened?"

"Oh," I said, remembering my black eye. "I ran into a door."

Sylvie just looked at me, then at Clio and Racey.

"She really did run into a door," Clio said.

"Hmm," said Sylvie. "Well. Anyway—are you guys doing something? Do you want to come sit with us?"

Suddenly I desperately wanted to go sit with them and pretend to be a normal high schooler. Stop worrying that every person I saw on the street was a potential threat, every step I took just bringing me toward a new danger. I glanced at Clio and Racey. Clio gave me a little nod.

"It's cool," she said. "I'll call you if I go to Ouida's, okay? But Racey and I can hang."

"Okay, great," I said, picking up my drink and cheesecake.

"Later," said Clio.

I grabbed a new table by the window while Sylvie, Claude, and the other guy went and ordered. A minute later they came back with their coffees.

"Oh, Thais, this is Kevin," Sylvie said. "Kevin LaTour. He goes to L'École too."

I smiled and nodded. "Yeah, I think I've seen you there."

"I *know* I've seen *you* there," said Kevin, smiling back. I blinked, realizing what he meant at the same time I realized he was pretty cute. He had a great, warm smile—bright against his dark skin. His eyes were a clear, olive green, and his black hair was twisted into little spikes all over his head.

"I loved having today off," said Sylvie. "School would be so much better if we always had three-day weeks."

"Hear, hear," said Claude, emptying a sugar packet into his coffee.

Just then Racey and Clio stopped by our table. "We're taking off," said Clio. "I'll call you later, okay?"

"Okay. And tell your mom thanks," I said to Racey. She nodded, and they left.

"Racey's mom patched me up my eye," I explained. "It happened at her house."

"Does it still hurt?" Sylvie asked.

"Not too much. Just looks stupid."

"Not too stupid," said Kevin. "How are you liking school here? You're from up north, right?"

"Connecticut," I said. "Um, I like school here okay. You know, it's school."

Sylvie nodded. "At least we only have eight more months. Yay."

"Then we get to do it all over again for four more years," Kevin said.

I made a face and laughed, and he laughed too. He was actually really, really cute. Of course, *cute* didn't even begin to sum up Luc's attraction, but still. The fact that I could even distinguish that about Kevin seemed healthy somehow. Good for me.

"Hey, we were thinking of hitting a matinee and then maybe going to Camellia Grill for a hamburger," Sylvie said. "You want to come with?"

I thought for just a second. Axelle almost never told me where she was going or when she'd be back, and I almost never told her anymore. The idea of being a free agent, just taking off and doing something like this without having to let anyone know, seemed great.

"Matinee'll be air-conditioned," Kevin coaxed.

"You talked me into it," I said, and he grinned. At that moment, I felt so happy to be sitting there, so un-witch-like, like I used to be.

Of course, I was kidding myself.

Éternalité

"This apartment is okay, isn't it?" Sophie asked Manon. She stood at the sink, washing their lunch dishes. Manon was at the kitchen table, reading the newspaper.

"It's fine," said Manon. "I like being on the second floor."

It had been lucky, how quickly they'd found a nice place to live, Sophie thought. The apartment wasn't big, just four rooms, but the two of them didn't need much space. And the building was charming, an old Victorian home that had been cut up and rented out. It was only a block from the streetcar line. Maybe if they stayed here awhile, they would rent a car.

Manon came up behind Sophie and put her arms around her waist. Sophie turned her head and smiled at her, still up to her elbows in suds. They didn't have a dishwasher, but she was used to that.

"Do you think Petra's twins will want to do the rite?" Manon asked her. "Want immortality?"

Sophie thought. "I don't know. Daedalus can't be making a good impression—he has 'power hungry' written all over him. And I don't know the girls at all. I just don't know. It wouldn't be an easy choice."

Manon was silent for a while, resting her head against Sophie's back.

"If you could choose this time, would you want it?" Manon asked. "Last time, we didn't get to choose. It got shoved down our throats. But do you think you'd have wanted it, *éternalité*, if you'd had a choice?"

"Hmm. I guess so," said Sophie, thinking. "There's been so much I enjoy doing. I like modern life. I'm so glad I've gotten to experience a life that isn't so hard and short, like it was when we were born."

"Also, it took you about a hundred years to fall in love with me," said Manon, and Sophie laughed, a little embarrassed.

"True," she said. "I was a slow learner."

"I wouldn't choose it," said Manon, letting go of Sophie and walking over to a window. "I wouldn't choose immortality."

Sophie was surprised. Manon had never said anything like that before.

"In fact," Manon said, looking out the window, "I've been doing a lot of thinking. If we can do the rite and change things, the way Daedalus says—I think I would choose to die this time. At last." She turned to look back at Sophie, but Sophie was frozen in place, shock turning her to stone.

Sophie had never, ever considered that Manon might want to *die*. The idea, after all this time, was unthinkable. They'd always been together, even before they were lovers. They'd always planned to be together in the future. Now, out of nowhere, she wanted to die? Sophie had no words. Without Manon—she would die also. There was no way she would want to continue in this life without Manon to come home to, to share everything with. They made each other laugh, comforted each other, held hands in scary movies. Took care of each other when they were sick. They were two halves, joined together. One half alone would never survive.

Carefully Sophie rinsed the plates and put them in the dish drainer. She couldn't remember the last time she'd felt so panicked, so desperate. Her heart was pounding, and cold sweat had broken out on her forehead. She couldn't even form the words yet to ask Manon why, why she'd want to leave her, to die. She couldn't even look at her.

But there was no way she would allow that to happen, no way she would let Manon die.

I ended up buying a pair of new shoes anyway. Racey and I hit our favorite shoe store on Magazine Street, and they had an adorable pair of Doc Martens on sale that would be great for what passed as winter here.

"Now what?" said Racey. "We've done the medicinal snack and the medicinal shoes. I for one am feeling a little better, though I never want to do magick with Thais again."

"Do you really think it's her?" I said. "But why would she have this effect? She hardly has any power yet. And it's not just because she isn't trained—I mean, I can do spells with some untrained little kid, and I wouldn't get blown across a fricking room."

"Well, I know it's not *me*," said Racey dryly.

For the hundred-and-oneth time I wished Nan was back, despite how upset I was with her, and that reminded me: I took out my phone and called Ouida's cell phone number. It rang, but in the end I only got her voice mail. I left a message, asking her to call me.

"Okay, so I'm going to take you up on your sleepover offer," I told Racey. "I just don't want to be in that house alone another night. Let me go home and get some stuff, and I'll come back later, okay?"

"Cool," said Racey, getting out of the car. "Later, then."

"Later."

I drove home, worry really starting to weigh me down. Just a few weeks ago, I'd been totally on top of my life. I'd met Andre, who was my soul mate and the guy I wanted to spend the rest of my life with; Nan was just my Nan; and everything was normal.

Now nothing was. I had an identical twin—me, gorgeous Clio, who all the guys stared at. I wasn't unique anymore. Nan wasn't really my grandmother, and she was part of some science-fiction setup with a bunch of other witches who made *Survivor* look like a tea party. Nan, my Nan, had lied to me my whole life. Everything I had thought was true about me and her had been a lie. It made me feel like I didn't know her, like I'd been living with a stranger. But . . . she was still my Nan, the only grown-up who always took care of me, and I couldn't help feeling like she was still the only person I could trust to keep me safe, especially with someone out there trying to hurt me and Thais. I shivered, automatically glancing in my rearview mirror at the thought. I knew just what Thais meant about feeling constantly on edge, like someone could be lurking anywhere, ready to come at you. It was beyond freaky to know someone wanted you dead and to have no idea who that person was.

I looked back at the road as I drove up to the

house, feeling relief wash over me when I spotted Nan's old Volvo parked three cars down. Finally, she was back!

Now I would get answers to my questions, hear her explanations. I leaped out of my car and raced through the gate and up the steps. Then Nan was opening the door for me. I hesitated for just a second—I was really angry at her—but old habits and my worry won out, and I threw myself into her arms.

"Nan!" I said. "Nan! I thought you were never coming back!"

She held me tightly, one hand stroking my hair, murmuring, "Shhh, shhh," the way she used to when I was little and I'd skinned my knee. And then, taking us both by surprise, I burst into tears. "Don't go away again," I sobbed, effectively leaving my calm, cool Clio image in the dust.

"I won't, my dear," Nan said. "Come inside now and tell me everything."

We went to the kitchen and I noticed she'd been home long enough to clean up. I watched her as she poured us cold drinks.

"You lied to me," I said, and saw her wince. "I trusted you. You've been lying to me my whole life. You kept my father from me. I'll never have a chance to know him."

"I'm so sorry, Clio," she said. "I was . . . afraid. I wanted to keep you safe, at almost any cost. I'm not sure if I did the right thing or not. But you have to believe that I never intended to hurt you."

"That wasn't even all, though," I went on. "Even

after all of that came out, and you barely explained it, then you go away and I hear about this whole Treize thing. It's . . . unbelievable. And I heard about it from a bunch of strangers. They were telling the truth, right?"

"Pretty much," Nan said quietly.

I let out a breath. Some part of me hadn't fully accepted it as real until that moment, hearing her confirm it. "You're not even my grandmother. We're related so far back I can't even figure it out!"

"Thirteen generations," Nan said, her long, slim fingers curled around her glass. "But we are related—I still am your nearest relative, besides Thais. And I wanted to tell you so many times, but I truly didn't know how. I just didn't want the Treize to touch your life."

"Too late," I said.

"I know. And I know they're putting their grand plan into action. You and I and Thais have to determine where we stand on that and on other things."

"Yeah, like whether we want to live *forever*," I said, and consternation crossed her face. I told her about Axelle and how we knew about the rite and had met everyone and had a circle.

"So you met Luc, did you?" Nan asked, as if picking up on something.

I shrugged. I'd never told Nan the details of my plunges into the dating pool, and now I felt even less close to her, trusted her less.

"Clio—did Luc hurt you? And Thais?"

There was no way I would admit how bad it had

been to anyone. It was too embarrassing and made me feel like my heart, pumping and bleeding, was hung on the outside of my chest.

I shrugged again and met Nan's eyes. "Not really." I sighed. "But what a jerk. He dated both me and Thais. Luckily, we found out almost right away. We both screamed at him, and then when we saw that he was also part of the Treize, we froze him out."

Nan looked at me, weighing my words. I wondered if she'd heard anything different, from someone else, and decided it didn't matter. That was my story, and I was sticking to it.

"So it wasn't any worse than that?"

"No. I mean, we're still majorly pissed. But we're dealing."

"Um-hmm."

I had to change the subject. "So where were you all this time? Why didn't you call?"

"I was in Connecticut, fixing Michel Allard's will."

I frowned. "Thais's dad?" I paused, feeling something weird in my stomach. "*My* dad?" I added, the words sounding funny. "Why? What do you mean, fix?"

"Somehow, right after Michel died, either Axelle or Daedalus changed Michel's will so Axelle would get custody of Thais."

"Oh yeah."

"Yes. So this time I went up and changed his will myself."

My head was spinning. "And they don't have phones in Connecticut? I didn't realize how backward they were."

Nan looked at me wryly. "I was extremely busy the whole time, and I didn't want to be in touch until everything was worked out. I knew you'd have so many questions. . . . The phone didn't seem the right way to do this."

"You changed the will back to how it was? Is Thais going back to Connecticut to be with that neighbor?"

"No. I changed his will so I would have custody," Nan said, her eyes very clear and calm, looking into mine. "I'm Thais's legal guardian now, and she's going to come live with us."

It took a moment for that to sink in. Another huge change in my life. I did feel a quick rush of gladness that she wasn't going back north, yet—

"Do I have to share my room?"

Nan smiled at me, so familiar, and despite my anger, I was relieved she was back. "No," she said, with an amused look. "I've thought about it, and I'm going to move myself to the little alcove room under the stairs. Thais will have my room. I don't need much space anyway. It will be fine."

Right now, the tiny little room under the stairs was our junk room.

"Well, if you think so. I'll help you clear it out," I said.

"Thank you."

And then here's the Clio part: it occurred to me that with Thais living here, I'd be much more involved with her life, know what she was doing. Like if she was seeing Luc, for example. I felt ashamed as soon as I thought that, but I knew it was true.

"Oh my God—there's stuff I haven't even told you," I said, my heart beating faster. "Someone's trying to kill me and Thais, and there's something wrong with Thais's magick."

Nan's eyes opened wide, and I went on to tell her all about our attacks, and the wasps, and how Melysa, one of my teachers, had saved us. I ran down our current theories and who we'd eliminated. Nan looked increasingly concerned as I went on, and her lips pressed together the way they did when she was mad at me.

Finally she nodded slowly, looking thoughtful. "Okay. I'm back, and I'll get to the bottom of that. Now, what do you mean, there's something wrong with Thais's magick?"

So I told her about the spells we'd tried, and how they'd gone wonky, and then we'd done the joining spell, which had blown us across the room. Nan had nodded approvingly at the mention of the spell, but when I mentioned the hand-grenade effect, she looked astonished.

"What?" she said, as if she hadn't heard right.

"We got blown right out of the circle, across the workroom," I said again. I told her how I'd set the spell up, putting in every detail I could think of. "I felt like a rag doll. Then, just this morning, I thought we could try to do a *réléver la griffe* to see if we could find out who was trying to hurt us."

Nan nodded; it was perfectly reasonable.

"We did it at Racey's because I felt weird here. And I set it up carefully, four stones of protection, blah blah blah, and I was doing my song, and Racey joined in like a million times before, and then Thais joined in, singing, and she sounded good, you know? Like she knew what she was doing. Or at least, like what was coming out of her mouth was real."

I realized I hadn't asked Thais how she'd known what to sing. I'd ask her later.

"Then what happened?"

"We got blown across the room. All of us. We felt like crap, and Thais hit her face on the cabinet. She has a black eye."

Nan looked at me like I'd announced I was joining the Peace Corps.

"I can't believe it," she said. "Racey got thrown too?"

I nodded. "And Azura felt it, a big boom of magick, inside their house, and she came running. She said not to mess with it again unless you were with us."

Nan shook her head. "You physically got moved, through a closed circle."

"We got thrown across the room," I repeated.

"Thais has a black eye? Where is she now?"

I shrugged. "She ran into some friends from school and was going to hang with them. Azura patched her up pretty good. It should be mostly gone by tomorrow. I mean, do you have any idea what could cause something like that?"

Nan didn't answer.

The Marked Girl Brings You Death

The snake—a non-poisonous boa constrictor—coiled around the fortune-teller's neck. Claire watched it, amused. It might actually spook someone who didn't know squat about snakes.

The tiny Thai woman, her face the color and texture of a dried tobacco leaf, peered down at Claire's palm very solemnly. Claire shot a glance at her friend, who'd convinced her to come see Madame Chu, one of the most respected fortune-tellers in Phuket. Her friend gave her a "be patient" glance and bent her head to light a cigarette.

This market was like any number of markets Claire had seen, in any number of countries. Uneven rows of canvas stalls, beat-up coolers holding fish, squid, shrimp. People hawking gold jewelry next to a stand selling fried batter. Roasted animals hung from poles overhead, filling the air with their scent and steam.

"What, Granny, she has no fortune?" Claire's friend joked at the ongoing silence.

Madame Chu looked up at Claire. "No, she has

too much." Her sharp black eyes, almost enclosed by folds of skin, examined Claire as if she'd just discovered an exotic new creature.

"Too much fortune?" Claire's friend laughed, the stall's single lantern casting shadows on her red cheongsam. "Lucky you."

"No," said Madame Chu. "Not lucky. Too much."

Claire laughed also, feeling the old woman's cool, dry hands holding her own.

Madame Chu bent low over Claire's hand. "Your fortune goes on and on," she said, speaking slowly. "Your time of death has come and gone. A dark one filled you with lightning, and now you live a walking death."

Claire quit laughing. "What?"

"Granny," said Claire's friend, frowning. "You are the best fortune-teller, I told her. Don't make me into a liar. Tell her the truth, and stop your nonsense."

Claire swallowed hard and wished she had a drink. Right after this, they would go to Samasan's bar. Absolutely. She'd paid up her tab and should be welcome again. Samasan never held a grudge.

Madame Chu's black beetle eyes regarded Claire over their hands.

"What else do you see?" Claire said offhandedly, as if she didn't care.

"I see a girl, marked—" The old woman touched her cheekbone. "Like a red lily flower."

Claire sat very still, her heart starting to beat faster. "She's dead," she said lightly. All of them died, sooner or later. Daughter after daughter after daughter.

"No." Madame Chu's eyes burned like coals. "She will kill you at last. The marked girl brings you death."

"Come on, Claire." Her friend sighed. "She's having an off night. We'll come back some other time, okay?"

Claire pulled her hand back and stood up, looking hard at Madame Chu. "Yeah," she said, throwing some money down. "It's all nonsense."

Madame Chu shook her head sadly, as if Claire were already dead.

Because of a funeral, a lot of the streets in the Quarter were blocked. After several frustrating minutes of circling blocks, I asked Sylvie to just drop me off and I would walk the rest of the way.

"You sure?" Sylvie asked.

"Yeah—you'll never get through. And I'm only four short blocks away from here."

"Okay, then. I'll see you at school tomorrow. Friday, yay."

"Yeah, okay." I opened my car door and started to get out. "Thanks a lot for bringing me along today. I had a great time."

"I'm so glad we ran into you," said Sylvie, and Claude nodded.

"I'll look for you at school tomorrow," said Kevin, and the look he gave me was more than a superficial, just-met-you glance.

"Um, okay," I said, and got out.

I waved goodbye and walked up the street, through the traffic barriers and in and out of the crowds of mourners. I had no idea who had died, but it was someone who rated a full-blown jazz-band parade, complete with umbrella walkers. I felt like an extra in a movie.

It was dark—after the movie we'd gone to Camellia Grill, which I loved. I'd had pecan waffles. Now it was almost eight o'clock, and I reviewed whether or not I had homework due tomorrow. The idea that I still had to think about homework, after everything I'd been through in the past few days, seemed crazy. But education waits for no one.

Kevin LaTour. He'd been really nice. Plus he was on the honor roll and was funny too. He seemed so much younger than Luc. Well, yeah, I guess he *was*—but even if Luc were only nineteen or so, the way he looked, Kevin still seemed much younger, still a kid.

But a nice kid.

And Sylvie was great, and she was so cute with her boyfriend. I was so glad that I knew them—a tiny island of normal sanity in my stormy life.

Even after I was out of the funeral, the streets were busy and well lit. In less than five minutes I was letting myself through the side gate at Axelle's. I hoped Luc wouldn't be there again. I didn't know how many more horrible, heartbreaking, dramatic scenes I could stand. None, actually.

Right before I put my key into the door lock, I heard raised voices from inside. I stood very still and listened, listened with all of me, not just my ears. I closed my eyes and pretended the words inside were little arrows, slipping right through the door. . . .

"How dare you!" That was Daedalus.

"You should have checked with her." Axelle. "You know she's happy here. I can't believe you would go behind my back like this!"

"It's unsupportable!" Daedalus sounded pompous, as usual. "It's a betrayal!"

"Oh, Daedalus, put a sock in it," said another voice. Petra! It was Petra!

I unlocked the door and rushed in. "Petra! You're back!"

Then she was hugging me, and I was hugging her back, my eyes closed, thinking of how incredibly glad I was, considering that really, I didn't know her all that well. But I belonged to her because my sister did.

Finally we separated, and she held me at arm's length and looked at me closely, examining my black eye.

"When did you get back?" I asked. "Does Clio know?"

"Yes, she does," said Petra, smiling. "I got back late this morning and saw Clio this afternoon. And now I'm seeing you."

"What happened to your eye?" Axelle said, coming closer.

"I . . . walked into a door," I said. I'd tell Petra the truth later.

Axelle's eyes narrowed, as if she knew I was lying. I didn't care.

"Oh, I'm glad you're back," I told Petra, and she smiled again.

"If I'd known I was going to get these enthusiastic welcomes, I would have gone away sooner," she said. "But I'm very glad to be back and to see you. And I have some news for you."

"Petra," Daedalus said warningly, but she ignored him.

"Are you hungry, Thais?" Axelle broke in. "Do you want something to drink?"

"What?" She'd never worried about that before.

"Listen," said Petra, putting her hands on my shoulders. "I've got some news. I was in Connecticut. I had your father's will changed so that I would have custody of you."

It took a moment for it to sink in. "Me? You have custody of me? How can you change a will?" Her blue-gray eyes looked into mine. "Oh. Magick." What a creepy thought.

"I'd like you to come home with me tonight," said Petra.

This was incredible—everything I'd hoped for.

"Thais—surely you don't want to leave," said Axelle.

I stared at her. Was she kidding? "I want to go live with Petra and Clio. Clio's my sister. And at least I'm related to Petra."

"Don't you want to stay? It hasn't been so bad, has it?" Axelle said coaxingly.

She actually wanted me to stay. I didn't think it was because she'd become fond of me. She had another reason, one I didn't know. And Daedalus was standing there looking furious. Clearly he wanted me here.

Well, that settled it. "Give me ten minutes to pack," I told Petra.

"Thais!" said Axelle.

"Look, you're right, it hasn't been that bad," I said to Axelle. Despite everything, I didn't want to be mean to her. "But—you know, it just feels more homey at Petra's. I want to be with my family." Plus I didn't want to be in the Quarter anymore, with Luc living maybe six blocks away. I dreaded running into him and would never go into my special secret garden again. "I'm sorry, Axelle. But I just want a regular kind of home." *And to live with someone I don't think could maybe be trying to kill me,* I added inwardly. Somehow I didn't really feel like it could be Axelle, but then again, I didn't know her very well. I didn't know any of them, really, but at least Clio and Petra were related to me!

Axelle glanced around at the chrome and black leather, the full ashtrays, the empty wine bottles on the counters. She looked as if she wanted to protest that this *was* a regular home but knew she didn't have a leg to stand on. "I wish you would stay, Thais." She gave me a smile, and Axelle is not a smiley kind of person. Even her cat would have known it was fake.

"I'm sorry," I said again, and went to my room.

It really did take only ten minutes to throw my stuff together. I had some cardboard boxes from my old house that I hadn't even unpacked, and my clothes fit into several suitcases. To my surprise, Richard came in while I was packing.

He leaned against the door frame, and his wide leather bracelet clicked against the wood. "Need some help?"

"Um—could you carry some of this out to Petra's car?"

"Yep." He picked up two heavy boxes as if they weighed nothing and left.

Twenty minutes later the car was loaded and Petra was driving us uptown to my new home.

"I'm so glad you're back," I said again. "So much has happened. Did Clio tell you everything?"

"I think so," said Petra, smiling at me. "But you tell me again. She said something strange happens when you make magick."

"You could say that," I said, gingerly touching my eye. I told her everything I could remember about the spells we had done and what had happened. She asked questions, and I answered them as best I could. "Do you know what's going on?" I asked.

Petra let out a sigh. "No, I actually don't. Perhaps it's the twin-power thing, though I hadn't expected your strength to be so reactive yet. But I'll look into it, sweetie. Now that I'm back, I'm going to try to get things more under control."

It was a comforting thought, and I felt even more comforted when we pulled up in front of their—my—house. I was going to live here. I felt like I was finally coming home.

"Am I going to be in Clio's room?" I asked as we started carrying my stuff up to the porch. "Or . . . on the couch?"

"No." Petra put down her load and went back to the car. I followed her. "Clio and I cleared out my room this afternoon. I've moved into the alcove room, under the stairs, and you'll have my room. You can repaint it if you want."

"What?" I was dumbstruck. "You gave up your room?" I was so touched by that and by her going to Connecticut to get custody of me. Tears welled up in my eyes and I sniffled.

Clio, I thought. Then the front door opened and Clio came out. I looked up at her, hoping she was okay with my moving in.

She smiled at me, not hugely effusive, but sincerely. "What a trip, huh?" she said, picking up one of my suitcases. "Oof. Glad to see you brought all your own personal bricks."

I laughed and Petra smiled, and it was right then that I felt like I really had a family.

That night I lay in my new bed, staring up at my new ceiling. My room at Axelle's had been long and narrow and kind of dark, with only one small window that was shaded by plants outside. This room wasn't big, smaller than my old room had been in Connecticut, but it was full of light in the daytime, with windows on two walls. It was painted light turquoise, which I thought I would keep, at least for a while. There was a painted border all around the room, about a foot from the ten-foot ceiling. It was painted in gold and was made up of a set of symbols, painted over and over again. Petra had explained that they were symbols of health and happiness, of peace and tranquility and magickal power. She'd told me their names, but I only remembered a few.

Now, as I lay with the moonlight shining bright through the Indian-print curtains, I closed my eyes and tried to feel whether there was any magick around me. The last couple of times we had tried doing spells, it had been awful and scary. But *I* was magickal, from a family of witches. Magick ran in my blood. I had just started to tap into it—I couldn't avoid it or pretend it wasn't there. It was like one of those party-favor flowers that blooms underwater, slowly unfolding and sending out colorful streams. It felt . . . different. I felt different. I felt like my life until now had been fine, even good, but that I'd been living under a layer of Saran Wrap, kind of. Now the wrap was slowly peeling off, showing me brighter colors, stronger flavors, fresher breezes. It was scary and weird, but also kind of exciting.

And here's the really strange thing, which I only realized just then: despite my mixed feelings about magick, despite being kind of afraid of it, I felt centered in myself. Before, it had been my dad who made me feel centered. The last couple of weeks, it had been knowing I had a real sister and Petra, who cared for me. But now I realized that somehow I felt connected and grounded all by myself, and I thought it was probably because of the magick. Like there was a magickal thread that kept me rooted to the earth, tapped into its ancient, unending life and power. I felt strong in myself in a way I hadn't before. Even though part of me wanted to keep away from magick, keep safe, a much larger part of me was being drawn to it, to its beauty and strength and goodness. I wanted to know more.

So Thais moved into Nan's room, and Nan moved into the tiny alcove room downstairs, where you could hardly stand up straight. I felt much less freaked and worried now that Nan was back, but in a way, having her right there was a constant reminder that she had betrayed me by not telling me the truth my whole life. It was hard. I loved her and depended on her, yet I was also kind of seething with resentment and anger.

I still thought of her as Nan, my grandmother, even though now I knew she wasn't. But I'd called her Nan for seventeen years, and it would be too weird to call her anything else. Still, something inside me felt like I couldn't trust her completely, the way I always had.

But with everything else going on, I knew I needed her more than ever now, even if I couldn't look at her the same way.

I also needed to get my mind off all this intense crap.

"Hey, I realized something," I said to Thais Friday morning. "My wardrobe just doubled. We're the exact same size. Now I've got twice as many clothes."

Always looking on the bright side, that's me. Actually, not really, but this *was* an upside.

Or not.

"Who's been buying your clothes?" I said, examining her closet critically.

"Me," she said, sounding defensive.

"Uh-huh." I stepped back and closed her closet door. "We must get you clothes that I'll actually want to borrow."

Thais gave me a sour look. Of course, she went to school wearing a layered tank top from the Clio Collection, so clearly she knew what I was talking about.

At school I waited while Thais gave her new address to the office.

She turned back with a smile. "It's official."

We pushed our fists together, then split up to go to our different homerooms. Her last name began with an *A*, mine with an *M*. I wondered if one of us should change.

So yeah, we were twins, and now we even lived together, but at lunch we still sat with our separate gangs. Racey, Della, Eugenie, Kris, and I sat outside on the sidewalk under the overhang, out of the sun. Thais sat with Sylvie and her boyfriend and a couple of other people over on the grass in the school's side yard. I noticed the same guy from Botanika sit next to Thais. Kevin something?

"Yo," said Trey, coming up to us. He dropped to one knee next to Racey.

Racey popped a few chips in her mouth. "Yo back."

"So. Collier Collier," said Della meaningfully. She tugged her miniskirt down an inch and leaned back against the building.

"Got any money?" Trey asked Racey.

"For lunch?" she asked him, and he shrugged.

"Go on," I said to Della. "Spill."

Racey rummaged in her purse. "All I have is a ten."

Trey plucked it from her fingers. "Ten-Q. Later."

Racey sighed and watched her little brother disappear. "That kid hits me up for more money. . . ."

"Race, Della's telling us what happened with Collier Collier," I said pointedly.

"Ooh," said Racey, sitting up. "Do tell. How's cradle robbing going?"

Della made a face at her, and Racey held up her hands. "What? He's younger than Trey!"

"That's 'cause Trey is only eleven months younger than you!" Della said. "You're like Irish twins!"

Racey rolled her eyes. "Go on. I'm all ears."

"He's really sweet," Della said, kind of lamely since she had all of our attention.

"Sweet?" I said.

"Yeah. He's just . . . really sweet. He doesn't take anything for granted," said Della. "Anything I do, he's all 'thank you' and everything."

"I bet." Kris smirked.

"No, I mean little things, like if I drive or ask him if he wants something to drink. He just doesn't take me for granted. It's really . . . different. Nice."

We all looked at her in silence.

Della sighed. "And okay, he's really hot too."

"Now we're talking," Eugenie said. "Are you teaching him everything?"

"He *knows* everything," Della said wryly. "If this is instinct, I'm all for it. That boy was made to please. He's . . . fabulous. Like he's made for me."

I knew how that felt. *Don't think about it.*

"Huh," Racey said, looking at Della speculatively. "Sounds serious."

"Oh, well, I don't know." Della picked up her soft drink can and drank from it. She seemed embarrassed, as if she hadn't mean to say so much.

I exchanged a look with Racey. Della was usually the love-'em-and–leave-'em girl, like me. Or at least, how I used to be. I'd never heard her say anyone was sweet before or talk about someone's actual personality. I looked around the school grounds and saw Collier Collier sitting with a bunch of sophomore guys. His eyes were on Della, and the puppy-love look on his face made my eyebrows raise.

How nice that some people had guys who were interested in them and only them.

"So, you know, if you want to borrow this car sometime, it's cool," I told Thais as I pulled up in front of our house.

"Oh, okay. Thanks," she said. "I don't even have a Louisiana driver's license. Guess I should get one."

I got out of the Camry and headed through the front gate. "Yeah. Then you won't have to use turn signals anymore."

Thais laughed, following me up the steps, and for

just a second I flashed on how different our lives would have been if we'd grown up together. We would have come home from school together just like this every day. And we would have hung out and fought over stuff and known each other really well. And either she wouldn't have known our dad or I wouldn't have had Nan.

I was putting my key in the lock when Thais said, "I wish you could have known Dad."

Just like that, out of the blue. One of those twin things, I guessed. I bit my lip. "Me too," I said softly.

Inside, Nan was waiting for us with Melysa, one of my teachers, in the kitchen. I hadn't seen Melysa since she'd saved our lives last week, and now I saw that she was checking us out for aftereffects.

"Ready to do some metal work?" Melysa asked me.

"Yeah—just let me grab something to eat," I said. "And that reminds me—I guess Thais won't be doing her rite of ascension, will she?"

Nan shook her head. "Not this year."

"Well, maybe by the time she's thirty," I said brightly, and Thais groaned.

Nan and Melysa laughed.

"What exactly is the rite of ascension, anyway?" Thais asked. "I've heard you mention it."

"It's a rite where a witch is tested on how much he or she knows on any number of given subjects," Nan explained. "About spellcraft skills, historical knowledge, decision-making abilities, and even just raw magickal ability."

"It's an incredibly important rite," Melysa clarified.

"Passing it, undergoing the process, greatly enhances your own personal power. Quite a few people don't pass it on the first try."

"So it's like the SATs," Thais said glumly, "but for witches. The WSATs."

"Yes, something like that," Melysa said, smiling. "I'm sure your time will come. But Clio's time is coming in only two months, so we better get to work."

"I'd like to learn more," said Thais hesitantly. "But it's been so weird lately. . . ."

"Actually, Thais, if it's okay, I'd like you to hold off working any spells for just a little while," said Nan. "You and I can start to go over some basic knowledge, though, about plants and properties of other elements. But I think you two shouldn't work any magick together until we figure out what's going on. Okay?"

"Okay," said Thais, and I thought she maybe even looked a little relieved.

I shrugged. "Okay."

That afternoon Melysa and I worked until it got dark—there were a couple of spells that are particularly effective right at dusk. She put me through my paces and I did really well, except for one little glitch where I accidentally wrote the wrong rune and had to start over.

But other than that, I did great—nothing went wrong.

Nothing got too big or weird.

I didn't get blown across the room.

So what did that say about Thais?

The Whole Balance of Power

"Hand me that magnifying glass, will you, Jules?" Daedalus held out his hand without looking up.

Jules got the small round lens from the shelf and handed it to Daedalus, who was leaning over a map on the worktable in Axelle's attic workroom. Downstairs he could hear Luc's raised voice, as if he and Axelle were arguing. He sighed. When Daedalus and he had first come up with this plan, it had sounded so feasible somehow.

"I'd forgotten how unwieldy the Treize is," he said.

"Hmm?" Daedalus glanced up. "Did you say something?"

Jules gestured to the door at the top of the stairs. "Sounds like Luc and Axelle are locking horns again. Somehow I'd forgotten how strong everyone's personalities are. Though I don't remember Luc being so . . . volatile."

"He never was," Daedalus said absently. Keeping one finger on the ancient map he was studying, he carefully wrote some notes in a small book. He stood up, capped his pen, and looked at Jules. "Luc's always gotten along with everyone—I mean, after Ouida got over their whole thing. We all knew Luc's foibles, but they never got in the way, never interfered with any of us. It's unusual, his being so . . . emotional."

"Sophie," said Jules, and Daedalus waved one hand dismissively.

"That's old news. It can't have anything to do with how he is now."

"So is it the girls, then?" Jules asked, frowning. "I don't see how it could be. His dalliances never—"

"Never reach his heart?" Daedalus laughed. "You're assuming he has a heart, Jules. You know Luc. He has a porcelain surface—nothing gets in, and nothing gets out. Yes, we'd discussed his plan, his mission, in regard to the twins. And it seems like he failed, which is certainly unique. But I can't believe whatever happened with Thais and Clio has affected him. There must be something else going on." Daedalus looked thoughtful. "Perhaps it would be prudent to find out what that is."

"Maybe he's against doing the rite?"

"No," said Daedalus, leaning over the map again. "Of course not. No, everyone is behind what we're doing."

"Not everyone," Jules said, frowning. "Remember—"

"No, everyone." Daedalus stood up straight again and fixed Jules with a glare. "No one could seriously oppose what I'm doing—you know that. Anyway, even if they did at first, they'll come around." He bent down to his work again. "Besides," he added, almost in an undertone, "even if they did, it wouldn't matter. None of them is at all powerful enough to really impede me. Well, maybe Petra."

Jules was stung. Maybe Petra? Only she? Pressing his lips together, he walked over to the gable window and looked out. From here he could see the river and hear the blare of tugboats' horns as they guided the huge tankers upstream. A haze hung over the water, and the last of the day's sunlight shone weakly through it.

Only Petra. Daedalus considered only Petra worthy of concern. So Jules's own power, own acquiescence, was taken for granted or not taken into account at all. And he noticed that this whole scheme, which he and Daedalus had developed together during the summer, now was Daedalus's plan, his idea. Who was Jules? An underling? An *assistant*?

Jules set his jaw, then schooled his face into calmness and turned back. His power. That was exactly what could change if they did this rite with the full Treize. The whole balance of power would change, in an instant.

Another Level of Desolation

"Bay," Richard murmured, painting it on his wall. The silver paint looked good against the deep blue, and he stood back to admire its effect. "'Wind.'"

Even though this apartment was only rented and even though he would no doubt not be here long, still, Richard had decided to go ahead and make his surroundings more comfy. His bedroom wasn't big, and his bed was a single mattress on the floor. A low altar in one corner was covered with red candle wax. But the rich blue walls felt good, and now he was painting silver symbols and runes in a border encircling the room.

"*Collet,*" he said, dipping his brush into the paint. He drew two small circles connected by a U shape. Necklace. A drop of silver paint dripped off his brush onto his bare chest. Absently he smeared it with a finger, then put down the brush and lit a cigarette. He was standing in the middle of the room, planning his design, when he heard the apartment door slam.

Richard grinned wryly. What a surprise—Luc was still in a bad mood. He heard cabinets open in the kitchen, liquid being poured into a glass.

Footsteps came down the hall, and then Luc was in the doorway, taking a sip of his drink.

"If that's the last of my scotch, I'm going to kick your ass," Richard said without heat.

"Left you some for breakfast tomorrow," Luc said, looking at Richard's handiwork. "You're going to have to repaint all this before you leave."

Richard shrugged, blew out some smoke, and tapped ash onto the floor.

Luc's eyes narrowed as he caught some of the symbols. "You doing something here, Riche, or is this just for looks?"

Richard glanced at him. "Looks."

Luc moved closer to the wall and tapped the symbol for feather. "*Plume? Collet? Tache?* If I didn't know better, I'd say you were working up to something."

Richard regarded him evenly. "Good thing you know better."

Luc drank, looking bleak. *Ah, the twins,* Richard thought. The lovely twins, with hair black as night, eyes green as the sea. Cerise's eyes. Armand's hair. Funny how their looks had been preserved so perfectly after all this time. Each daughter, daughter after daughter after daughter, had married. Some had married men in the *famille,* some had married outsiders. But for all that inpouring of genetic material, here the twins were, almost identical replicas of Cerise. As if they had sprung from her directly, without their blood being watered down over and over. His mouth set in a grim line and he went to pull on a T-shirt, carefully switching his cigarette from hand to hand.

"So you know Petra's back," he said.

Luc looked up. "Really? When? Where was she?"

"Got back yesterday. Apparently she was up north, refixing Michel Allard's will."

"In what way?" Luc asked.

Richard took a drag on his cigarette, acting casual, drawing out Luc's torment. "She got custody of Thais. Plucked her out of Axelle's like a chicken out of a fox den. But you probably know this." He watched Luc out of the corner of one eye, saw him run a hand through hair already ragged, his face achieving yet another level of desolation.

"Thais isn't at Axelle's anymore?" Luc asked, trying to sound calm and failing. Richard frowned. Luc actually seemed to have it bad, which was disturbing. Okay, fine, fool around with them, not a problem. But something more? It could be . . . dangerous.

Richard and Luc had always gotten along, as long as neither hampered the other in getting what he wanted. So far they'd never wanted the same thing.

"Nope," Richard said, putting out his cigarette. He screwed the paint cap back onto the jar and set it aside. "She moved uptown with Petra last night. I helped load the car." He looked at Luc thoughtfully. "If they told Petra about you screwing them both, she's going to have your blood."

Luc flushed. "I didn't screw either one of them."

"Sorry. I meant screw over."

"Bite me." Luc's hand was clenching his glass so hard Richard thought it might break.

Richard smiled. "And you would call it . . . ?"

"A mistake." Luc turned away, heading down the hall to the kitchen. Richard followed him, saw him dump the last of the bottle into his glass and slam it down.

"So much for breakfast tomorrow," Richard said. He leaned against the counter. "I've never seen you like this. And your uncharacteristic lack of finesse in this situation has raised eyebrows. What's going on?" He laughed. "Oh, *déesse,* don't tell me you actually care."

Luc's face hardened. "Like you should talk," he said, quietly biting. "The way you used to moon over Cerise. The whole village knew. They thought it was funny. Too bad she wasn't interested in a little kid."

Richard felt anger heat his blood and tried to quench it. His throat hurt and he swallowed hard, wishing like hell Luc hadn't just drunk the last liquor in the house.

"What makes you think she wasn't interested?" he said mildly. "Anyway, let's just say my technique has improved in the last two hundred years. As has my success rate. Since the twins have given you the brush-off, would you mind if I had a go? How about Clio?"

"Good luck," Luc said bitterly, staring at his empty glass. "She's a handful."

Richard kept his eyes on Luc. "Or maybe Thais?"

Luc looked up, and Richard was surprised, though he didn't show it. He'd seen Luc in every situation there was, from crazed drunken revelry to the bitter ashes of regret, but he'd never seen this, this cold, weirdly calm look of murderous rage.

"Try it and I'll rip your heart out," Luc said.

Maybe Another Two Hundred Years

"They told you this?" Ouida asked, and Petra nodded.

Morning sunlight shone in through the plants hanging in front of the window. It cast green-tinged dappled light over the table, the worn linoleum of the floor. Petra opened the back door to let more breeze in.

"Récolte soon, and as hot as July," she murmured.

"This is New Orleans," Ouida said dryly. "Monvoile will come and go and it'll be as hot as July. But maybe you're not used to it yet. Maybe another two hundred years."

"Should be cooler by Soliver," Sophie said. "Maybe."

A noise by the screen door made Petra look, and Q-Tip smacked the screen with one paw.

"Oh. Present for Mommy," Ouida said, looking through the screen.

"Ick," said Sophie. "Is that a mouse?"

"What's left of one," Petra said with a sigh. She opened the door and let Q-Tip in, then held out her hand. "*Tranquillez*," she murmured, sketching a quick sign in the air, and the cat froze in mid-step on the kitchen floor.

"Why does that work if he's deaf?" Ouida asked.

"I don't know," said Petra, kneeling by him. "But I'm glad it does. Okay, Q-Tip, drop the mouse. *Laissez tomber.*"

Q-Tip's mouth opened, and the mouse corpse fell onto the floor.

"It's a lovely mouse, Q-Tip," Petra said, getting a plastic baggie. "Thank you so much." She patted his head, and though he stayed in place, she felt him start to purr. "You are such a good hunter. A fierce and mighty hunter. I'll put this mouse somewhere safe. *Déchargez.*"

Q-Tip, released from his holding spell, sat down and started washing his paw.

Petra put the mouse baggie up on the counter to get rid of later.

"Okay, where were we?" she said, sitting down again.

"Where you were telling us that someone's trying to harm Thais and Clio," said Sophie.

"Yes," said Petra. "And I believe them." She described the different attacks the twins had told her about. "But they said it hasn't happened lately—not since the circle with the Treize, in fact. Which is why I let them go out to do some errands today. Did either of you feel anything that night? Anything off or dangerous?"

"You mean besides Daedalus?" Ouida asked.

"The girls were angry at Luc," Sophie said stiffly. "Really angry. And there was more strong emotion, going between all three of them."

Petra nodded. "Yes. I have to talk to him. Each of them says things with Luc were superficial—that they're angry but dealing. Did you get more than that?"

"Oh yes," Sophie said, frowning. "I feel sure—there was much bigger stuff between them, big, strong emotions." She shook her head, her lips tight.

Petra thought. Why hadn't the girls told her this? Embarrassed? She looked at Sophie. "Has he told you anything about what happened between them?"

"We don't really talk," Sophie said, twisting a ring around one finger.

"Sophie," said Ouida gently. "It's been too long, *cher*."

Sophie looked at Ouida, her eyes wide. "How can you say that? *You*—"

Ouida reached out to put her hand on Sophie's. "It was a very long time ago. He was young and foolish and selfish. I've made my peace with him. He's a different person now, and so am I."

Sophie didn't look up. "We just don't get along."

Across the table, Petra met Ouida's eyes. *Drop it,* she told her silently. *You'll get nowhere.*

"Okay, so we have someone trying to harm or possibly even kill the twins," said Petra. "We have the Luc thing, which I'll get to the bottom of. We have Daedalus and his rite. Where do you two stand on that?"

"I don't want to do it," Sophie said, surprising Petra. She still didn't meet Petra's eyes, which meant she was hiding something.

"I'm not sure," Ouida said slowly. "My first reaction was no way. But as I think about it, I wonder if it could be used to sort of, well, heal things. Heal *us*."

Petra nodded. "I know what you mean. Personally, I don't trust Daedalus. I'm not sure how I feel about the rite. I can see both sides. Thais and Clio haven't told me what they would decide, and I still need to figure out how hurting them would benefit anyone, or benefit or hurt the rite."

"It would hurt *you*," said Ouida. "And we need both of them to do the rite, to be thirteen."

"So it could be someone who wants to specifically hurt Petra but in an emotional way, not a physical way. Or it could be someone who doesn't want the rite to happen," said Sophie. "I mean, besides me. *I'm* not trying to hurt the twins."

Petra nodded again. "I know. I just can't figure it out. The girls did a *rélever la griffe* but got nowhere. I'm going to have to work on it. In the meantime, I've been thinking about the rite, and it seems like it would be prudent to get, well, insurance, in a way. Something on our side so Daedalus can't pull the rug out from under us. Here's what I was thinking." She outlined her plan, and both Ouida and Sophie nodded thoughtfully.

"I agree," said Ouida. "That's a good idea. I'll help you."

"Me too," said Sophie. "It can't hurt, and it would be good if we get it."

"Okay, then." Petra sat back in her chair. "We'll go tomorrow. Then . . . there is one more thing," she said slowly, wondering if she should even bring it up. She felt Ouida and Sophie watching her and decided to take a chance. "The thing is . . . Thais is starting to learn a bit of magick. She's worked a little with Clio and also with me. And . . . almost every time, her magick goes big and unpredictable."

Ouida frowned. "What? In what way?"

"It's hard to say," Petra continued. "In a way I haven't seen before. It happens fast. And—they've told me—twice, in the middle of a spell, they've actually gotten blown across a room. Through a circle and physically across the room."

Her two friends stared at her.

"Nooo," Ouida said doubtfully, and Petra nodded.

"I talked to Azura Copeland—the mother of one of Clio's friends. She was in her house when the girls were out in the their workroom, in the backyard. And from inside the house, she felt a big clap of magick, like lightning, and when she ran out there, the three of them were lying on the floor, in separate corners, stunned."

"But just ordinary magick?" Sophie asked, looking concerned. "Nothing dark, nothing . . . dangerous?"

Petra shook her head. "No. I even did a *reléver la griffe* on Clio. Nothing dark came up at all. They were working relatively small, totally ordinary spells. And then, when Clio was working much harder and bigger spells with Melysa, everything was fine."

"What are you saying?" asked Ouida. "You think it's something about Thais?"

Petra hated what was coming next, but she really needed their input. "What if . . . what if . . . Thais is a dark twin?"

Petra saw Ouida blink, saw Sophie's eyes widen.

"Oh God," Ouida said, a look of dismay on her face.

"That doesn't happen very often," Sophie said. "I mean, I've never known anyone—"

"I know it's rare. And I'm hoping it's impossible," said Petra grimly. "But how they're describing Thais's magick—what else could it be?"

"I've met her," said Ouida. "I didn't pick up on anything dark from her at all."

"Me neither," said Sophie.

Petra shrugged, feeling hopeless. "She might not know it. Not yet. For seventeen years nothing magickal has touched her. Now she's starting to tap into her powers for the first time. Maybe a crack has appeared in her. Maybe it's getting worse."

Ouida shook her head. "I just don't know. They both felt balanced to me, in the short time I was around them. They both had elements of light and dark, mostly light."

"I know," said Petra. "I feel that too. And I don't really know how a dark twin works. I've heard that it's when the one egg splits, and instead of it separating into two even halves, with both positive and negative forces, one twin gets all the light and one gets all the dark."

"Which would be bad," said Sophie.

"Not irredeemable," said Petra. "Not one hundred percent inevitable, but often bad and always a struggle."

Ouida looked up at her. "You just moved her into your house."

"I know. And I'm praying I'm wrong. Most likely

I am," said Petra. "But can you help me, keep an eye on her, get close to her, try to pick up on anything?"

Ouida nodded, looking upset.

"All right," said Sophie. "I'll try."

"Thanks. And whatever happens, do not tell anyone else about this. No one. Understood?"

Sophie and Ouida nodded, then the three of them sat lost in thought. The only sound was the rhythmic click of the ceiling fan, going around.

On Saturday Clio and I did errands together, hitting the plant store, returning a pair of shoes. I looked out the car window, still learning how New Orleans looked and smelled and felt. Huge live-oak trees lined St. Charles Avenue, which was where the main streetcar line ran. The tree branches almost met over the center of the median, making an incredibly green, lush tunnel to drive through. Dad would have loved it. Maybe he'd seen it before.

Dad. I still missed him so much. Despite everything that had happened, there were a hundred times every day when I turned to say something to him, wanted to ask him something, wondered when he would be home for dinner.

He hadn't looked much like me. His hair had been dark, but mine was darker. He'd had brown eyes. But he'd felt so totally mine, my blood father, the one constant in my life since I was born. Realizing all over again that Clio had never known him was sad. I decided I would make her a little scrapbook, with pictures of him in it, and I would write about him in the pages so she would know him.

"Well, can you choose just one thing to work with?" I asked Clio.

It was almost dinnertime, and we were sitting at the kitchen table. Petra—I still didn't call her Nan; it felt too strange—hadn't come home yet.

"Yeah," she said. "A lot of people have a favorite assortment of materials to work with, like if they have a special affinity for herbs or crystals or metals. And you can do powerful spells with just those. But Nan always said that the best spells, the strongest ones, are balanced, with elements of each. Though there are also some spells that specifically don't need crystals or herbs or candles or whatever."

"And you know everything about all this?" I felt dismayed by how ignorant I was, how much I had to learn.

Clio grinned. "Not everything. Talking to you helps me realize how much I actually do know. But I've been studying this since I was really little. You'll catch up."

This was so depressing. "It's like every plant in the world has some use." I groaned. "How can I learn them all? I mean, *trig* is too much for me."

"Me too," Clio said. "But with magickal things, it's like any other subject—you learn it a little bit at a time. And yes, many, many plants in the world can be put to some kind of magickal use or have certain attributes. Pretty much everything does. Every grain of sand, every drop of rain, blah, blah, blah. Magick is in everything, yours for the taking. And then of course, certain human-made objects can also be very powerful."

"Uh-huh," I said glumly. "Like, give me a plant example."

Clio looked around, thinking. "Okay, something easy and common. Holly."

"Like we have outside? Christmas holly?"

"Actually, we call it Soliver holly," Clio told me. "Soliver is our winter holiday. In Wicca it's called Yule. Yule log, et cetera. At roughly the same time, the Christians have Christmas. Jews have Hanukkah."

"I'm a Christian, sort of," I said. "We don't have Christmas?" This was not good news.

Clio looked at me like I was an idiot. "We have Soliver," she said patiently. "It's a lot of fun. It'll be okay. Very festive. Do you want to know about holly or not?"

I sighed. "Tell me."

"Okay, holly." Clio looked at the ceiling, thinking. "The broad Latin name is *ilex*. You learn the Latin name because it'll be the same in most languages. It's the scientific name and helps you be precise. Then you have its true name, which for the kind of holly we have outside, but not for other types, is *bestgriel*. You use its true name in some kinds of magick. It's considered a masculine plant, not because it actually has a gender, though it does, but because its properties align along the masculine scale. The element associated with holly is fire, our element. Which would make it a bit more effective or appropriate for us than for someone whose element is something else. Mars is the planet associated with it, so certain spells can take Mars's orbit or properties into account. And mostly, holly is used for protection, all sorts of protection. And good luck. At Soliver we decorate the house with it, and it helps us have good luck in the coming year."

Until now, my main knowledge about holly had been "prickers." "And you know this kind of info about a lot of plants?"

"I better. It's going to be a big part of my rite of ascension."

I breathed out. "So maybe when I'm thirty."

"Maybe." Clio looked smug, but not in a mean way. I decided to change the subject.

"You know who's good-looking? Kevin LaTour."

"Sylvie's friend?" Clio considered it. "Yeah. He is. You hung out with him the other day, right?"

"And Sylvie and Claude. Kevin seems nice, too."

"I've never talked to him." She looked at me speculatively. "Are you . . . interested in him?"

There it was again. The unspoken gulf between us. Luc. I hadn't told her a lot of how I felt about him, and she had her secrets too, I was sure. They'd probably even slept together, but I didn't let myself think about it, because it made me feel sick.

Anyway, Luc was behind me. I was moving on, facing the future. A future without him.

"*Interested* is a strong word," I said cautiously. "I've just noticed that he's nice and also really good-looking."

"Yeah. Well, more power to you if you like Kevin."

I looked into her eyes, identical to mine, as if I might see what she was thinking behind them. Was she hoping I would forget about Luc? Did she still want him? I looked away.

I shrugged. "We'll see."

We worked silently for a few minutes, each with her own thoughts.

"Do you think there's something wrong with me?" I hadn't meant to ask the question, but it just popped out.

"In a general sense or just your clothes?"

I made a face at her, and she smirked. "I mean my magick. Is it just because I have no idea what I'm doing? Do spells go that wrong very often?"

"No. Hardly at all that I've heard of," said Clio, more seriously. "I mean, maybe they won't work or they'll work but in a skewed way. But getting knocked out of a circle? Doesn't happen."

"So it's just me, then. Something about me." That idea upset me, even though I still hadn't totally embraced *Bonne Magie* as a way of life.

"Hmm," said Clio, looking at me.

"What?"

"I just remembered a spell I heard of once," Clio said thoughtfully. "It was, like, to see someone's aura. I mean, during a circle, you can usually see everyone's auras, and some people can see them on other people all the time, just walking around. But I remember reading about a spell where it reveals a person's inner state, like an x-ray of your soul. Sort of. I remember thinking it was pointless because people usually know their inner state and express it if it's good—if it's bad, they wouldn't do the spell in the first place and let anyone see."

"Uh-huh," I said. "You mean you want to do that with me? Nan said we shouldn't—"

"Nan said we shouldn't try any twin-magick magick," said Clio, standing up and heading to the workroom. "But this would be more diagnostic. Besides, we'll do it outside so we won't get thrown into a wall. Your eye's finally better—don't want to do *that* again."

Out in the backyard, Clio cleared a little space on the brick walkway that wound through the foliage, much like Racey's backyard. There were six-foot wooden fences on both sides and a brick one in the back.

It had taken Clio almost half an hour to find the spell and assemble what we needed. Now she set up a brass bowl the size of a cantaloupe and kindled a small fire in it. I was worried that Petra would come home and be mad about this, but she hadn't returned yet. Clio told me that it wasn't unusual for Petra to miss a meal if she was at a birthing.

Clio drew a circle around us with salt, then took a chunk of broken red-clay brick and drew different symbols on the walkways around us. "This is *épine*," she said, drawing a vertical line with a little triangle on one side. "It's to help us achieve our goal. This is *ouine*." She drew what looked like a pointy letter *p*. "It's for success and happiness. *Porte* is for revealing hidden things."

I recognized that one from the spell we had done at Racey's house.

"*Ôte* is all about one's ancestral birthright," Clio explained, drawing the symbol on the ground. "It's about what you've inherited, and it can mean personal or material things. Okay, I think we're about ready."

"No candles? No incense? What about those four little cups?"

"We don't always use those," Clio said, sitting down across from me. "This one is aimed differently."

"Okay."

As with the other spells we'd ever done, we sat facing each other, holding hands on either side of the little fire bowl. The sun was setting. It was hot and humid.

I was afraid to do this. I didn't know what would happen, and I dreaded feeling that blast of magick in my chest like before. And even the smaller spells we'd done had spiraled out of control and been scary. I was tentatively getting used to feeling the spark of magick in me and even kind of liking it. But actually doing something with it was so much scarier. What was I doing?

"It'll be okay," Clio said confidently, as if she could read my mind. "But this time, don't say anything, or sing, or do anything, okay? I'll do it."

"Okay." I tried to calm my breathing and relax, but it was hard. It seemed to take forever before I felt myself unwind. I closed my eyes. I tried to open myself to the world, like Clio had said, but I didn't even know what that felt like.

And then I did. I felt the "magickal" essence rising in me, as if a peony were blooming, unfolding inside my chest. I felt happy, peaceful—calm and excited at the same time. I was part of everything, and everything was part of me. Clio and I were connected, and I'd never felt so whole or complete. Was this because we'd done the joining spell?

I vaguely heard Clio chanting, singing a spell in a soft voice. My hands and knees were a little warm from the tiny fire kindled in the brass pot. Clio's fingers tightened on mine, and just like that, we were off.

Suddenly I felt like I was trapped on a roller coaster that was speeding recklessly around a track that I couldn't see ahead of me. My eyes popped open and all I saw was Clio's face, *my* face, looking scared. Was she seeing my soul, my aura? Could she tell what was wrong with me?

Then we were seeing images, flashed in front of us like before, when we'd had the swamp vision. This was very similar—only this time, I knew who most of the people were. We saw Petra, looking younger than she did now, arguing with a black-haired man. He turned and stormed away from her, and we saw that he had our birthmark on one cheek. We saw Richard, not tattooed and pierced and gothicky, but looking happier, more innocent, and dressed like he was in a colonial movie. He was chasing a girl through a meadow, and she fell, laughing. Richard fell next to her, and then they were rolling through the tall grass, kissing wildly, her hair flying bright against the birthmark on her cheek. With a gasp I recognized her. This happy, laughing girl, so full of life, was the same girl from our other vision—the one who had died in childbirth at the witches' circle. I could see her face still and gray in the rain, the ground beneath her running scarlet. It was only then that I realized she looked almost exactly like Clio. Like me.

The scene shifted abruptly, making me almost motion sick. None of this seemed to be about the spell Clio had cast. I didn't know why we were seeing any of this. We saw another woman, dark-haired, running through a moonless swamp. Her face was beautiful and cruel, her eyes black. She looked behind her, and then we saw her lying facedown in the shallow water, her bare feet stained with mud. There was a dark figure over her, a man, holding something in one hand. A tool? A scythe or an ax? Had he killed her?

Then once again we saw a huge multi-forked bolt of lightning split a huge tree. The witches in the circle were almost knocked off their feet, and the tree was on fire, burning brightly. I could hear the hissing as the rain hit the fire, sending up tiny jets of smoke.

The tree's fire was so hot I felt it on my face, uncomfortably warm and too bright to watch. I tried to pull back, but Clio was gripping my hands tightly. I blinked and saw her face red with heat, flames dancing all around her. Her eyes were wide and still, unfocused, and somehow that made me more afraid than anything.

"Clio!" I yelled, shaking my hands, locked in hers. "Clio!" I pulled back as hard as I could, knocking us both to one side, and all of a sudden we were lying on the ground in Clio's backyard. I'd broken the spell. It was nighttime, the sky above me dark and speckled with stars and . . . sparks, flying upward? I jumped to my feet.

"Oh God, Clio!" I yelled, looking past her. I grabbed her shoulder and shook her—she hadn't sat up yet. Now she blinked slowly, looking at me like I was a stranger.

"Clio! Get up! The house is on fire!" I shouted, shaking her hard enough to rattle her bones. With the next breath she seemed to awaken, sitting up quickly and looking around her. She gasped and put her hand over her mouth, as horrified as I was.

This time we hadn't gotten thrown across a room.

We'd started a fire that had leaped away from us, and our house, my new home, was ablaze.

First Thais was shaking me, her face pale but brightly lit. She was yelling something, but I couldn't hear it. She shook my shoulders hard, and then I made out the word *fire*!

That woke me up, and I was back in the now. I jumped to my feet and stared, horrified—the whole back half of our house was engulfed in flames.

"Oh, holy sh—where's a phone?" I cried, my brain feeling scrambled. I had to think, get two thoughts together—

Just then, one of the back windows burst from the heat. We were ten feet away but felt crystalline shards of window hissing against us.

"Thais! Go next door! Call 911!" I shouted. I was amazed the fire trucks weren't already here—the fire was huge and must have been burning for at least twenty minutes. It was night; I had no idea what time.

"I can't!" Thais cried, pointing. "The fire!" I looked and saw that she was right—like many New Orleans houses, ours was on a tiny plot of land. The fences separating us from our neighbors were only about six feet from each side of the house. The flames were already billowing out on the sides—you couldn't get past them. The wooden fences had just caught on fire too.

I spun, thinking. Six-foot wooden fences, six-foot brick fences. I'd never climbed over them, and it looked like it would be a bitch to try. Thais was watching me anxiously: her fearless leader.

"Under the house," I said.

"What?"

I was already moving forward. "We have to go under the house," I explained quickly, dropping to my knees. Our house was built up on brick pilings, maybe three feet up, in case the river flooded. Most houses were. So there was a crawl space beneath it.

"The fire is mostly higher," I said, crawling toward the house. "Under the house isn't on fire yet. We have to get through out to the street, and then we can call 911."

"What if it collapses?" Thais almost shrieked.

"Move fast," I said through gritted teeth. This close to the house, the fire was so hot it felt like it was scalding my skin. I hunkered down lower and bellied under the house, having to crawl over a water pipe and a natural-gas pipe that went to our stove. *Oh, crap,* I thought. *If the fire gets to the gas pipe—*

"Come on!" I yelled back to Thais, and saw that she was biting her lip and creeping low to the ground, right behind me. Quickly I muttered an all-purpose protection spell. Oddly, my studies hadn't included a specific spell for keeping a burning house from falling on you.

I hadn't been under here since I was eight, when

I had been hiding and found a rat skeleton. And I wished I hadn't thought of that just now.

Above me, I heard the hungry crackling and roaring of the fire as it happily, eagerly consumed our walls. More glass broke and I winced, though it couldn't reach us under here. I was crawling as fast as I could through the fine, cool dust under the house, inhaling it up my nose, smelling smoke everywhere. Every couple of feet we had to crawl around pipes or wiring. I felt Thais following me, and then I saw the light of the front yard just ahead.

"We're almost there," I shouted, and scrabbled right out next to the front steps, through the holly bush. I knelt and waited for Thais, and she crawled out a second later, her pale skin showing whitely through her grime.

"Okay, you go next door and call 911," I said. "I'm going to call Nan and Melysa and anyone else who can help!"

Thais nodded and turned to run—then we both heard an anguished howling coming from inside the house.

"Q-Tip!" Thais gasped.

"Holy mother—he's inside the house!" I said. "Wait!"

But Thais had already run down the narrow alley between the house and fence. The fire was still mostly toward the back third of the house, but windows were breaking and I feared an explosion at any second.

"Thais!" I yelled again, but she was running

along, looking up at the side windows. At the third window in, the one in the workroom, she stopped. I saw the dim whiteness of Q-Tip's fur pressed against the screen in the open window. Before I could think of what to do, Thais jumped up and punched a hole right through the window screen. Q-Tip shot out and raced down the alley toward the street. He streaked through our front fence.

"He'll be okay," I said, grabbing Thais's arm. "Let's go!"

As we were running through the front gate, I heard the droning of sirens, coming nearer. Thank the goddess, someone had called the fire department.

The huge red fire engine stopped abruptly in front of our house. I noticed that neighbors were starting to come out of their houses to see what was happening. Thais and I were on the front sidewalk, and I realized I was shaking. I put my arm around Thais, and she put hers around me.

"Out of the way, miss!" shouted a firefighter as he started pulling loops of flat canvas hose off the truck.

Then it was like watching a movie. Thais and I had to move out of the way as several firefighters surged past us, the hose on their shoulders.

"Is anyone inside?" one yelled to me, and I shook my head. "No!" I was so thankful Q-Tip was safe. He was probably under the house across the street. Then I had a paralyzing thought.

"Nan's books!" I gasped. "Her tools!"

"Oh no!" Thais said, her face dismayed. "She's going to kill us! Maybe we can—" She looked up at the front porch.

"The fire probably hasn't reached the workroom inside," I said slowly. "Maybe if I run in and you catch them as I toss them out the window . . ."

"Girls! Please!" said a firefighter, making us jump. "Get across the street! Now!"

Thais and I looked at each other, then reluctantly moved across the street. I could throw a glamour so that they wouldn't notice me going up the front steps. I could—no. It was stupid. Nan would kill me for taking the chance. And if I happened to blow myself up doing it—I would be grounded forever.

Then I heard the hissing spray of fire hoses and saw great clouds of billowing smoke rising as they began to extinguish the flames. Nan's beautiful garden in front had been trampled, her tomato stakes knocked over, her herbs crushed by the heavy water hoses.

"How did this happen?" I asked, my throat closing. Tears burned my eyes, which were full of smoke and ash.

"I don't know," said Thais, her voice trembling. "But I guess—I guess it was me," she said so softly I could hardly hear her.

I looked at her. "Oh no," I said. "It was just—I'm sure it was—" But the truth was, I couldn't reassure her. I actually couldn't be sure it *wasn't* Thais. Nothing like this had ever happened to me before she came.

I don't know how long we stayed there, watching our fire slowly be vanquished. There were two fire trucks and three hoses hooked up to the fire hydrant down the block. The street was full of our neighbors, who kept coming over to see if we were okay or needed anything or when Nan would be home. Someone brought us glasses of iced tea, which felt incredibly good on our scorched throats.

Finally the fire was out. The firefighters began coiling their hoses. Thais and I stared numbly at our house. Just from the front, it looked okay, except for the ruined garden. But in back—the whole back half of the house was scorched, and at least four windows were broken. We had no idea what the inside would be like.

We were still standing there when Nan ran up to us. She'd had to leave her Volvo down the block because of the trucks.

"Oh my God!" she cried. "What happened? Are you all right?"

I nodded, feeling close to tears again. I hated crying, but maybe it would help make Nan more sympathetic? I tried a practice sniffle.

"There was, uh, a fire," Thais said hesitantly.

"Ma'am? Is this your house?" The fire chief stood there, looking hot and sweaty.

"Yes. What happened?" Nan asked anxiously, stepping over to him.

"Well, the back of your house got torched," the fire chief said bluntly.

"How?" Nan exclaimed, then quickly turned to me. "Did someone try to—?"

She was asking if this had been another attack on us. The temptation to shout, Yes! and have someone else take the blame was almost overpowering. And Nan had lied to *me*.

"No," said Thais, before I could finish thinking it through. "At least, we don't think so." She met my eyes quickly, then went on. "I mean, it could have been. It's hard to know. But there's a chance . . . we started it."

Nan just stared at her, trying to take it in. Then she turned to the fire chief.

"Can you tell how it was started?" she asked.

"We almost always can," he answered, taking off his hat and rubbing his sleeve across his forehead. "And our specialist is still checking it out. But I've had twenty-five years of experience, and I've never seen anything like this."

"Like what?" Nan asked faintly.

"It looks like someone threw a . . . sheet of fire directly at the back of your house," he said, frowning, as if he knew his words didn't make a lot of sense. "I mean, fires always start in one place, then spread. Or if an accelerant is used, there's a traceable pattern. The back of your house looks like someone sprayed it with gasoline, then threw a match at it."

Nan put her hand over mouth and drew me close. Then she put her other arm around Thais.

"But the thing is, so far there's no trace of accelerant," he went on. "There's nothing to suggest that it was deliberately set. Except for the fact that its pattern simply can't be natural."

He shook his hat against the side of his waders and called to his men to finish loading.

"You should contact your insurance company,

ma'am," he said. "And when I get the final report from our specialist, I'll send you a copy. Or the police will want to conduct a further investigation." He made a sympathetic face, then strode toward one fire truck, barking orders.

"We were doing a spell," I confessed in a tiny voice. "In the backyard. I was trying to see Thais's aura, to see if I could tell why her magick always goes weird. But we saw that same tree get hit by lightning and catch on fire, and the next thing we knew, the whole back of the house had gone up." I really did feel like crying now. "I'm so sorry, Nan. We didn't mean to do it. I don't know why it happened."

She nodded, looking tired, and tucked a stray strand of hair back into her loose bun. She looked up quickly. "Q-Tip!"

"We got him out," Thais said.

"Thais got him out," I clarified. "She punched a hole in the screen to rescue him."

Nan took Thais's hand and looked at the scratches the metal screen had caused. Then, putting her arms around us both again, she started toward the house.

"I'm so thankful neither of you was hurt," she said.

They've Seen What Happened

"But they weren't hurt?" Ouida asked, looking back at Petra in her rearview mirror.

"No," Petra said. "They went to school today, but their hands and faces look sunburned."

"And you don't know how it happened?" Sophie asked.

"They were doing a spell," said Petra. She closed her eyes and leaned against her seat back, glad that Ouida was driving. She felt like she had aged more in the last seventeen years with Clio than she had in the two hundred years before that. "A spell to see what might be causing Thais's magick to explode."

"I'm sorry," said Ouida. "How's your house?"

"Water damaged, from the fire trucks," said Petra, wishing she could block the picture of her charred house from her mind. "The whole back of the house went up. It'll need to be scraped and sanded and painted and maybe a quarter of the weatherboards replaced. The windows are cracked and need new glass. Inside, the house smells like a smoke pit. Thais and Clio stayed up late, trying to mop up the water in the kitchen, but it's going to take weeks to get the house back to normal."

She opened her eyes and saw Ouida looking at her in the mirror.

"Do you think this lends credence to your dark-twin theory?" she asked.

"I don't know," said Petra, feeling worn out. First that difficult birth all day and then coming home to find her house on fire. Clio had been upset about not being able to save Petra's books and tools, as if she would care about those things. And they hadn't been touched anyway. Her first, panicked thought had been that someone else had set the fire, trying to harm the girls. But it didn't seem like that was the case.

"Why don't you try to get some rest?" Ouida suggested. "I'll wake you up when we get to Chacahoula."

"Maybe I should." Petra looked out the car window, thinking. "You know, the girls have shared visions of that night, the Treize, by the tree, with Melita. They've described the action as if they were there."

Sophie turned around in her seat, horrified. "*Pas vraiment!* But how could they?"

"I don't know," Petra answered. "But they've *seen* what happened. More than once. Really seen it—the rain, the power surge, the lightning. Cerise." Even after all this time, it was a fresh pain, the memory of her daughter. Since then, Petra had tried to help as many other women give birth as she could. "And last night, they saw someone facedown in a swamp and a dark figure standing over her, holding something, some kind of weapon. Thais described her as dark-haired, black-eyed, and beautiful."

"Not Axelle," said Ouida.

"No. Axelle's best friend."

"Melita?" Sophie asked. "They saw her dead?"

"I don't know if she was dead," Petra said slowly. "Clio just said she was facedown and someone was standing over her. And it was clearly a scene of danger. Maybe she *was* killed that night—or maybe just threatened or injured? I don't see how she could have died. . . ."

"Daedalus thinks there's a chance the rite affected Melita differently somehow," Ouida said. "He thinks there's a small chance that she wasn't made immortal. But that seems so improbable."

"Impossible," Sophie said, frowning.

"But she did disappear that night, without a trace," said Petra. "Without taking any of her things—not that she had much."

"Who was standing over her?" Ouida asked.

"I don't know, and neither do the twins. They think it was a man, but the figure was very dark, completely in shadow. They couldn't describe him at all."

"Petra," said Ouida seriously, "don't tell anyone else about the girls' visions."

They met eyes in the mirror, warm brown looking into blue-gray.

"I know," said Petra. If anyone else knew the twins

were having these kinds of visions and if these visions had revealed or would reveal the answers to centuries-old mysteries, then the twins would definitely be in danger, perhaps from someone else and for a different reason than they were now. Petra sighed, rubbing her hand over her eyes. If that even made sense. She could hardly think, could hardly sort out what made sense. Had the girls set the house on fire? Or had someone seen them performing a spell and taken advantage of that to set the fire himself? Or herself?

Why did the girls seem to have more than two hundred years' worth of memories locked inside them? Could they remember all twelve generations of ancestors, back to Cerise? Why?

And was Thais a dark twin? Petra had questioned Clio separately last night. It had been very late. Petra had helped Clio make some aloe ointment for her and Thais. Clio had explained the point of the spell, and Petra had asked her what she'd seen. Clio had described the same thing that Thais had, yet Petra was certain that Clio had seen something else, something that had disturbed her, that she wouldn't talk about.

It was a problem. Her life was becoming layered with problems.

"Petra," Sophie said gently. "We're here."

Groggily Petra opened her eyes. Through the open car window, she saw tall live-oak trees blocking out the sky. Gray wisps of Spanish moss trailed down like tattered silk. In an instant, Petra was taken back to another time, when she would look overhead and see nothing but trees and sky and moss. No buildings, no planes, no wires.

She'd liked their little village. She'd grown up there. Even its name, Ville du Bois, Village of the Woods, reflected how simple and innocent their lives were there. Not easy—never easy—but still, rhythmic and uncomplicated. Predictable, but in a good way. Crops, farm animals, knowing the plants, the birds in the wood, the fish in the streams. The cycles of *Bonne Magie* tied in so beautifully, so naturally. It took more effort to feel connected to the earth, to nature nowadays.

She'd grown to be a woman there. She'd married Armand, whom she'd known all her life. They'd had children. Melita. Jacques had died when he was two. Philippe had lived ten months. After that she'd decided to have no more children. But accidents happen, even to witches performing anti-fertile spells. That had been Cerise, born when Petra was almost forty. Cerise had been a joy, never a sick day in her life, and Petra had taken another chance. But Amanda had lived barely long enough to be named and blessed.

Then Armand had tired of village life. He'd gone on a trip to New Orleans to buy tools and lead to make bullets. He'd come home only once—to ask Petra to take the children and move with him to the city. She'd been afraid. She hadn't wanted anything to happen to her daughters.

Very ironic.

She knew that Armand had died of malaria when he was forty-five. She'd seen his headstone in the cemetery in New Orleans. Where she now lived. After having lost her last two surviving children to disastrous circumstances.

"Petra?"

Petra blinked and looked up into Sophie's face, as smooth and unlined as when she'd been twenty. Sophie looked concerned, and Petra sat up and opened the car door.

"Sorry," she said, climbing out of the car. "Wool gathering."

She looked around. They were parked on a narrow shell road that was used so rarely that grass had sprung up in the tracks. "Where are we?"

Ouida waved at the map spread on the trunk of the car.

"Here," said Sophie, pointing to a spot. "Bit southeast of Chacahoula. We left the main roads about forty minutes ago."

"Get a bit of a rest?" Ouida asked.

"Yes." Petra squared her shoulders. "I can face this now."

"I miss Boston," Ouida grumbled, wiping the sweat off her brow.

Petra smiled at her, then pushed her own damp hair off her forehead. September was bad enough in the city, but in the middle of the woods, right on the edge of the swamp, it was suffocating.

"You can't just breathe," Ouida said. "You have to actually *swallow* the air. That's how thick it is."

"I miss Paris," said Sophie.

"You and Manon will be able to go back there soon enough," Petra reassured her.

"Yes . . ." said Sophie.

Ouida checked her compass. She looked overhead, looked again at the detailed topographical map she'd gotten from the extension service. "Well, as close as I can figure, we're about here."

Petra looked around, but nothing was familiar. The trees here had been mostly cleared out, probably a hundred years ago. New growth had sprung up, nature reclaiming its own.

"Okay," she said, pulling some supplies out of her dress pocket. "We might as well give it a go."

"It's creepy being here," Sophie said. She glanced over her shoulder as if waiting for someone to spring out of the woods. The light here was filtered and dim, and the only sounds were from insects and birds.

The three women quickly made a circle on the ground, then stood inside it, holding hands. Petra felt a heaviness weighing on her that was more than the heat and the humidity. Damn Daedalus! When he'd brought Thais to New Orleans, he'd opened up a viper's nest. Now snake after snake was slithering out, weaving paths of danger all around both Clio and Thais. The twins had almost been killed several times. Thank the goddess Melysa had been home the night of the wasp attack. Now Petra's own house was a wet, blackened reminder that something was seriously out of balance in her life.

"Petra?" Sophie's voice was gentle.

"Sorry." Petra closed her eyes and breathed out slowly, trying to release every bit of tension, fear, and dread. Finally, finally, she felt herself slip into that place between waking and dream, where her boundaries blurred and merged with everything around her. She felt Ouida's breathing, heard Sophie's heart beating, felt their energies, older now and shaped forever by their lives, but still beautiful. She began her song of power and magick, softly at first, resting lightly on the air. Soon she was joined by Sophie, then Ouida, the three of them weaving their chants together as if they were fine threads being spun into a strong, silken rope.

Within her, Petra felt her power rise, felt her magick strengthening. A slight trembling shook the earth below their feet, and Petra's eyes opened. Their voices didn't waver, but they looked at each other. The whole Louisiana delta was made of layers upon layers of clay and river silt. There were never earthquakes here.

Petra gasped slightly, feeling like a huge hand was pulling the power right out of her chest. She felt Ouida and Sophie squeeze her hands harder, and she closed her eyes again and tried to stay centered.

Their voices rose in a strong, feminine crescendo, and at last the song was over and they broke apart from each other, staggering back. The trembling stopped.

The world looked different. It felt different.

The air was tinged with the scent of rain, and purple clouds swelled overhead. A thin cool wisp of breeze brushed Petra's face as she looked around in the much dimmer light.

"Storm coming in," said Ouida, sounding breathless.

"Yes," said Petra, feeling resignation settle on her.

"Look," Sophie whispered, and Petra and Ouida turned to her. Sophie's face was white, her eyes dark and troubled. One hand was outstretched, pointing, and Petra squinted to see.

"There," Sophie said, her voice shaking.

Then Petra saw it. Ouida's mapmaking had proven true. The three women looked at each other, a mix of emotions on their faces.

"It's still here," Ouida said disbelievingly. "I never thought that would work."

Petra's lips were pressed together hard as they walked over to a small clearing right past the first line of trees. There, on the ground, was a blackened ring of scorched earth, a circle of ashes. Where Cerise had died that night.

"We've found the Source," Sophie said sadly.

"It wasn't your fault," Clio said again. "Well, I mean, probably. I mean, you totally didn't mean for anything like that to happen."

I made a wry face at her, tied the top on a bag of apples, and put them in the cart. School had been miserable today. Clio and I both obviously smelled like smoke—everything in our house did, including our entire wardrobes, and we hadn't had time to wash any clothes. My face and hands still stung slightly despite Petra's soothing ointment. Now we were at the grocery store. Petra had left the house early this morning, saying she had a case, and asked us to stop and get some things.

"You want some nectarines?" Clio asked.

"Yeah. A bunch. I love 'em." Sighing, I picked out three baking potatoes and put them in a bag. I felt wiped out, stressed and upset and tired. Of course it had been almost impossible to sleep last night. Also, since my bedroom was the top back one, all my windows were broken and the window frames scorched on the inside. My curtains had burned away, and the whole room had been drenched with water. I'd slept on the floor in Clio's room.

My throat felt tight. I brushed some hair out of my eyes. I had finally found a home, a home full of love and acceptance, and wham! I'd almost burned it down. My own room, which Petra had given up for me—

I swallowed and tried to remember whether we had anything green in the fridge at . . . home.

"You can't blame yourself," Clio said, seeing my face. "We're just not sure." She lowered her voice as we pushed the cart forward. "I mean, how do we know it wasn't like Nan said, that maybe someone saw us doing the spell and seized the opportunity to set the house on fire? You know that's possible."

I nodded and let out a deep breath. "Yeah, that's true." But inside, I couldn't help feeling it had been me, something about my magick.

"Are we out of mayonnaise?" Clio asked, pronouncing it "my-nez."

"Close to it," I said.

"Do we need bread?"

I nodded. "It got . . . toasted." Clio and I looked at each other, and at the same moment, we burst out laughing.

"Oh God, that was awful," she said, laughing.

"I know. But it's true," I said, still giggling. "The plastic was burned off and the bread inside was all . . . toasted." I felt much better after we had laughed, but I still had heavy thoughts on my mind. "Clio—there must be something wrong with me. Maybe I'm . . .

like, bad or something. Like Melita. Maybe I'm not supposed to make magick."

"No, Thais, don't be silly. They said that Melita was evil. You're not evil. You're not even a little bad. I don't know what's wrong with your magick, but I know it's not *you*. We'll fix it. Nan will fix it. Just be patient."

"I mean, I think I like magick," I said, putting a big can of coffee in the cart. I was used to coffee with chicory now. "Sometimes I think it feels really good. Not like a drug or something unnatural. Not like I'm ecstatic. But just that I feel really calm and connected and strong."

Clio smiled at me. "That's what magick is."

"But then it goes weird, and it's big and scary and I hate it." I shook my head. "I don't know what to do. Maybe I should forget about it." But even as I said that, I realized that I didn't want to now. Maybe a week ago I could have given magick up, never tasted it again. But now something in me was pulling me forward, eager to explore it. The whole thing worried me and made me feel anxious. I hoped that Petra would be back by the time we got home, but then I remembered what that home would look like, smell like, and a weight of depression settled on me.

"Do Petra's cases always take all day?" I asked.

Clio shook her head. "Nope. Sometimes they're really fast. One time she left at noon and was back by three. But they usually take longer."

"Okay. You have the card?"

Clio pulled out her bank card, and we pushed the cart into the checkout line.

Two normal teenagers picking up stuff for dinner. Two ancestral witches, tied to a line of immortals, with combined explosive magick, who someone kept trying to kill, picking up stuff for dinner.

My life had gotten so complicated.

My fingernails would never be clean or unbroken again.

After the fire had been put out on Saturday, Nan, Thais, and I had glumly cataloged what work needed to be done on the house. Fortunately, insurance would cover a lot of it, but not all. Some of it we would have to hire someone for. And Thais and I had to do as much of it as possible. Which we were doing after school and in any spare time.

The outside of the house in back had to be scraped and sanded and repainted. Some of the charred boards had to be completely replaced. The linoleum in the kitchen had to be pulled up because water had gotten under it and would rot the wooden floor beneath it. We had to cut it into pieces, muscle it out of the house, roll it up and tie it, and put it out on the curb for the trash guys to pick up. It was so horrible. We'd done that yesterday after we got back from the store.

Almost every cupboard had to be emptied, everything inside it washed and dried, then put back. The cupboards and even the walls had to be scrubbed to get off the soot and grime and water stains. About half of Nan's plants that hung in the windows had died. We had to clean the rest of them. We'd only been at work three days, and I felt like I'd be doing this for the rest of my life.

"I guess I'll be repainting my room after all," said Thais. She was sitting on the floor, scrubbing the kitchen table legs, which were also covered in oily soot. "And getting new curtains."

"Yep. Did you switch that load of clothes into the dryer and start a new load?"

"Yep. Poor Petra, having to go this late."

I glanced at the clock—it was almost nine. Nan had left an hour ago on a case. I climbed up another step on the ladder so I could clean the ceiling fan. "Midwives don't really keep predictable hours."

The doorbell rang. At this hour? I froze, looking at Thais, my heart rate speeding up. Then I realized that someone trying to murder us probably wouldn't *ring the doorbell.* Relaxing, I tried to feel who was there. "It's Jules—and Richard, I think. Did you know they were coming over?"

Thais shook her head. "You think it's okay?"

I thought as I climbed down from the ladder. "I guess so." But I still felt uneasy. Just then the phone rang, and Thais answered it. She held up one finger for me to wait, and the doorbell rang again.

"Oh, okay," she said, her face clearing. "Actually, they just got here." She motioned at me to go answer the door. "When do you think you'll be home? Okay. No, we're fine. 'Bye."

She ran to catch up with me just as I was reaching the door.

"That was Petra," Thais said in a whisper. "She asked Richard and Jules to come replace the glass in the windows. I guess they know how."

"How conveeenient," I said, and opened the door.

Jules nodded at us and gave a restrained smile. "Hello. Hear you have some windows need reglazing." His voice was deep, all the edges smoothed out by his southern accent.

"Yep," I said, gesturing them inside.

Richard held up a package of windowpanes wrapped in brown paper. "You have a hissy fit?" he asked, throwing his cigarette down on the porch and grinding it out with his boot. "Throw a shoe through a window?"

He was so incredibly irritating. I wished I could say something scathing, but he was here to help, which we needed. He looked me up and down, which was so bizarre coming from someone who looked several years younger than me, and I was suddenly conscious of how grimy and filthy I was.

I forced myself to meet his eyes calmly. "We set the house on fire. Busted the back windows."

His look of quickly masked surprise was intensely gratifying.

"It's late," Thais said, leading them through the house. "Would this be easier to do in the daytime?"

"Yes," said Jules. "But we might as well do it now before it rains again. Sorry we couldn't come earlier—Petra only called us today."

"That's okay," I said. "We appreciate your helping." I glanced quickly at Richard to find him watching me, one eyebrow raised. I set my teeth and moved the butcher-block thing out of the way so they could get to the back window. Jules took my ladder and went outside, and Richard stayed inside. They set to work removing all the jagged hunks of glass still in the frames, and I got some newspapers to wrap them in.

"Thanks, babe," Richard said absently, not even looking at me.

I glared at his back, then looked down at Thais, who was trying not to snicker. I joined her under the table and started washing another table leg.

After the table, Thais began washing plants in the sink, and I started on one of the bottom cupboards. Most of the top ones had been done, thank God. I opened it and pulled everything out, mostly baking pans, which I could run through the dishwasher. I got a new bowl of hot soapy water, leaned way in, and started washing down the sooty walls.

The smoke had even gotten inside the fricking cabinets, I thought angrily, scrubbing away. I wrung out my rag and ducked back in. Inside *closed cabinets.* Smoke could get into everything. All of our clothes had to be washed—we were almost done with that. All the curtains in the whole house needed to be washed, the upholstered furniture taken outside and beaten and vacuumed and aired. The smell of smoke and ash was everywhere, permeated everything. I was sick of it. And it had been all my fault—mine and

Thais's. That was the worst part. I couldn't even resent anyone else.

I was swearing to myself, rubbing furiously away, when someone touched my bare foot. I shrieked and banged my head against the top of the cupboard. "*Damn* it!" I pulled my head out of the cabinet to see Richard squatting on his heels in front of me, trying not to grin. A lit cigarette dangled from one hand. I looked at him, unable to keep the anger off my face.

"Put that out," I said curtly, sliding out to sit on the floor. "Nan doesn't let anyone smoke in the house."

"I understand," Richard said, taking a puff and blowing it toward the stained ceiling. "You don't want the house to smell all smoky." His dark brown eyes looked like they were challenging me. "Next you'll be telling me it's bad for my health."

My eyes narrowed at him. I didn't care if he *was* helping—he irritated the piss out of me. "*Your* health isn't the problem," I said, sounding snippy even to myself. "But Thais and I still have just the two, no-lifetime-warranty sets of lungs. So give us a break."

After a moment Richard smiled as if to say, Point to you. He stood up and put his cigarette out in the sink. I felt uncomfortable and didn't know why. Richard didn't feel dangerous—but he set me on edge, kept me off balance in an incredibly annoying way. I felt too aware of my dirty tank top and short cutoffs that barely covered my underwear.

"Where's Thais?" I asked.

He motioned toward the back door with his

head. "Outside, picking up glass. We're all done." His hair was too long and cut all raggedy, as if he'd done it himself. The natural color was the same warm brown as his eyes, but it was streaky with different shades of blond. His eyebrow ring was gone, but he had a small silver wire through one side of his nose and three earrings in one ear and two in the other. One of them was way on the top of his ear. He was wearing a black T-shirt with the sleeves torn off, showing the tribal tattoos on his upper arms. The cloth was so old and worn it had a comet tail of holes spread across his stomach. I could see smooth tan skin through the holes, and then I realized what I was doing and looked up quickly.

Damn, damn, *damn*. He was watching me examining him, and he had that half-amused smile on his face.

"Like what you see?" he said, almost sounding teasing.

"Oh, *right*," I said sarcastically, standing up and brushing off my shorts, completely without result. In the next instant he stepped toward me, and I looked up in surprise. He was only a couple of inches taller than me, inches shorter than Luc. I was so taken aback I froze, and he deliberately put one hand on my waist and pulled me to him. Then he lowered his head, watching my eyes, and kissed me. His lips were warm on mine, firm and gentle, and I had the utterly insane, unbelievable thought of *yes*.

In the next second I pushed him back, hard, and put my hand to my mouth, horrified. Just then the back screen door opened, and Thais came in, looking filthy and exhausted. Jules was behind her, carrying his box of tools, as cool and unruffled as when he'd arrived.

"That window's fixed," he said, nodding toward the one on the back wall. "This one has cracked panes, but nothing that can't wait till tomorrow. I've stapled plastic over the windows upstairs in case it rains. Tomorrow I'll get an earlier start and finish them all up." He looked over at Richard, who was standing unsmiling by the sink. "You ready, Riche?"

Richard nodded and flicked me a glance, then walked out of the kitchen. I let Thais show them out and make all the grateful noises—I was too freaked to deal. Oh my God, Richard had kissed me. I mean, I'd been ducking unwanted kisses since I was twelve—I knew how to avoid them. How had he gotten to me? Was I just so surprised I—

I waited till I heard the front door close, then headed into the hallway where the stairs were. "You look wiped," I told Thais. "Go ahead and take a shower first."

She nodded tiredly and headed upstairs.

I sat down on the bottom step, my chin in my hand. I couldn't *stand* Richard. Andre—Luc—was the only person I wanted to kiss, the only kiss I wanted to remember. Now Richard had changed that. I knew how he'd felt when he'd held me to him, knew how he kissed.

Damn him.

Undermine All Their Plans

A cool shower. That was what she needed. A cool shower, some Tylenol, some food, and she would feel fine.

Axelle glanced at her watch as she opened her front door. Not much past ten. Thais would be home, maybe already in bed. Inside the apartment, she dropped her purse on the table. Minou trotted up and rubbed against her legs.

"What's the matter?" Axelle murmured. "Thais didn't fee—"

Axelle sighed. Right, no more Thais. She went to put food in Minou's bowl, which she had to find first. Then she opened a bottle of water and rummaged for the Tylenol in a cupboard. She took four of them and washed them down with Pellegrino.

The refrigerator revealed no food. Which would have been fine and normal if Axelle hadn't gotten used to Thais keeping the fridge full of yogurt and interesting cheese and sliced ham and even eggs.

Axelle found half a box of Frosted Mini-Wheats in a cupboard and took them to the living room. She flopped down on the couch, opened the box, and crunched some up dry. With each one her chewing became angrier. This was pathetic! She was pathetic! She'd gotten along all this time with no Thais, no one, and it had been *fine*. Was she going to fall apart now that Petra had stolen Thais away? Not bloody likely. Axelle stood up and threw down the box. She would take a shower, change, and go out for real food. Tons of restaurants stayed open all night. Or she could order in.

She lit a cigarette and blew the smoke across the room. The fact was, she kind of missed Thais. Not that Thais had been a barrel of laughs. Just the opposite. She'd covered the dining table with boring schoolbooks and made pained expressions when Axelle left clothes on the floor. Clio, the other one, would have been much more fun. She would have liked going to bars, while Thais whined about being underage. She would have been fun to shop with, whereas Thais seemed content with her boring, schoolgirl clothes.

But Thais had been something new and interesting in Axelle's life—the first time Axelle had had even a superficial resemblance of responsibility for someone else. Maybe she hadn't done such a great job—she wasn't some TV mom. But still, had it been so bad that Thais should run off to Petra's the first chance she got?

Damn Petra anyway. She thought she had the right, that she knew best, that she could just undermine Axelle and Daedalus and all their plans. Fine. Take Thais. It didn't change anything. Everything was still going forward as planned.

Axelle found herself in the hall in back of the kitchen, standing in the doorway of Thais's room. She had saved Thais's life! Had she remembered that when she'd been racing out to Petra's car? No.

Axelle had thought about that night a lot but still wasn't sure who'd been behind the magickal attack on Thais. She knew it wasn't Daedalus or Jules—they both wanted, needed the twins to do the rite. They were all hell-bent on doing the rite, like it was some big magick party where everyone would get a prize. Maybe they didn't remember what it had been like, had felt like that night. How could they have forgotten? It had felt terrible, like death. Some of the secret magick Axelle had worked with Melita so long ago had been scary, left nasty hangovers. But nothing had ever felt as bad as that night.

And Cerise has died, leaving behind baby Hélène, a pretty thing. Everyone expected Petra to raise her, but she'd been adopted by Louise and Charles Dedouard.

Axelle picked up one of her wooden cups. After Thais left, Axelle had put them on the little desk in Thais's room. She smiled wryly, remembering when she'd found them in Thais's bathroom, one holding swabs, one holding cotton balls. . . .

The wood was cool and smooth. Axelle rubbed it on her black silk shirt, making the wood shine. The grain of the wood was thin and straight—the tree had been hundreds of years old. Jules had carved these for her out of the charred stump of the Source tree. Maybe he'd felt sorry for her, with Melita being gone.

They'd been like sisters. Much more like sisters than Melita and Cerise. Cerise had been a bubble-headed idiot who'd gotten herself knocked up when everyone knew how to prevent it. And why hadn't the father prevented it, if he was a witch? Men could do it too.

Unless the father hadn't been a witch. Or had wanted the baby for some reason.

Axelle put the cup down next to its mates. Jules used to make nice things. That was one of the first things anyone noticed about him, that he could make pretty things out of wood. That and the shackles on his wrists and ankles.

No one in their *famille* had ever owned another human being. It was bizarre, unthinkable. Why would the slave owners do that to themselves? They were probably *still* working out the bad karma.

Marcel had found Jules, Axelle remembered. Almost dead, in the swamp. A runaway. Marcel had brought him to the village and given him to Petra, who was a healer even then. It had taken a month of magick and nursing to bring Jules back to this side of life. The blacksmith had broken the shackles. He'd actually melted them down and made them into an iron knife, and he'd given it to Jules. Axelle couldn't remember his name.

Then Jules was just one of them, one of their *famille*. He made himself a little house, he learned their religion, he got work as a carpenter. But it was the little things, the pretty things he carved, that Axelle had always liked best. Jules had changed a great deal over the years.

Sighing with the weight of memories, Axelle went back to the kitchen and started opening cupboards. Richard seemed to have cleaned out all her liquor. Ah! She found a bottle of dry vermouth with maybe a quarter left and poured herself some over ice.

No, owning slaves had never been acceptable in their religion, their clan.

Which was why Luc had caused such a brouhaha when he'd come back from New Orleans, owning Ouida.

Luc's family, the Martins, had been well-off. Petra would have been well-off too if Armand hadn't taken all their money when he moved to New Orleans. Armand's brother, Luc's father, had sent Luc off to Loyola, in New Orleans, to get a college education. Luc had lasted two years before being sent down for behavior unseemly in a gentleman. Big surprise there. He'd had angry fathers coming after him with shotguns when he was fourteen. Luc's father had been incensed. Then Luc had shown up, cocky as hell, owning a female slave.

Axelle laughed softly, remembering how the entire village had been in an uproar. What a scandal. Luc was lucky no one had beaten him to death. He and his father, Gregoire, had had a huge row, right out in the village commons, and Gregoire had publicly divested him of ownership. Ouida was free to stay or go as she pleased.

Ouida had stunned everybody by choosing to stay—with Luc. Just for a couple of months until she figured out what to do. She could have headed north, where not many people owned slaves, or gone to Europe. Luc's father would have given her the money. But Ouida made friends in the community. Petra and Sophie started teaching her the ways of *Bonne Magie*. Like Jules, Ouida had quickly made a place for herself.

Then she'd decided to see something else of the world and had left. But she had returned, and that time, she'd stayed and become one of them.

It had been around then that Sophie had cut Luc out. Axelle had heard rumors but still wasn't sure of the real reason—Sophie had never said why, and neither had Luc. The *famille* had many secrets, and that was just one more of them. Axelle leaned against the kitchen counter and drained her glass. She felt better. Now for a cold shower, and she'd be ready for anything.

It was a shame about Sophie and Luc, Axelle thought as she walked toward her bedroom. They'd been such a handsome pair.

Axelle paused halfway through the main room. She frowned, standing very still. There was an electricity in the air, a heightened sense of... what? Very slowly and quietly Axelle walked the perimeter of the room, trying to feel where it was coming from. Outside, on the street? From the courtyard in back? Had someone spelled her apartment? All her senses sharpened. Then she passed the hidden door that led to her attic workroom. It was open about a quarter of an inch—the latch hadn't quite caught.

Quickly she draped a shadow spell over herself to

make it hard for anyone to pick up on her presence. Leaning closer to the door, she slid one long red fingernail into the crack and pulled. The door opened a fraction, enough for her to hear voices.

It was Jules and Daedalus—but she hadn't felt them when she'd come in. They had a key and came and went as they liked, but why hadn't she instantly known they were there?

"Luc?" She heard Jules ask.

"No," Daedalus said impatiently. "He's strong but completely unreliable."

"Not Petra, obviously."

"Obviously."

"Richard?"

"Yes, maybe Richard," Daedalus said, sounding thoughtful. "Possibly Richard."

"There's Axelle," said Jules.

"Please, no," Daedalus said. "Axelle is fine in many respects, but not for this. We need someone more focused, with more true power. Axelle has let herself grow weak."

Axelle's perfect eyebrows arched. Oh, really? Her magick had gotten weak, had it?

"She has other priorities is all," said Jules.

"Which are not our priorities," said Daedalus firmly. "No, Axelle is out. I wonder if Manon . . ." His voice trailed off, and Axelle could no longer make out their murmuring.

Quietly Axelle backed away from the door, picked up her purse, and let herself out of the apartment. She closed the door soundlessly and went to stand in the dark, covered carriageway that ran alongside the apartment. Leaning against the smooth, cool stucco, she thought.

Well, it was true. She had let her magick grow weak. She'd never been a scholar, a student—instead of learning everything there was to know, she tended to learn only the aspects that would let her perform certain spells. And what was wrong with that?

Besides, she'd thought that she, Daedalus, and Jules were a triangle, an even-sided balance of power behind this whole rite. But they were planning something, the two of them, something they hadn't shared with her. Perhaps she wasn't as tight with Jules and Daedalus as she'd thought. Perhaps she needed to look out for herself more, protect herself more. Yes, Daedalus was very strong, but so was Petra, so was Richard, and so was Luc, when he focused on it.

More than one allegiance could be made.

Daedalus had been so convincing about how this rite would answer everyone's needs, even if they differed, but suddenly Axelle wasn't so sure of that. Certainly Daedalus's needs would be answered—he would make certain of that. And anyone whose desires aligned with his would be well served also.

But not everyone wanted the same thing. What Axelle needed to do was really figure out what she herself wanted out of this. Then she would work with whoever could help her get it.

Now, with a plan in place, she headed back to the apartment. This time she let the front door slam shut and made a lot of noise walking around the big room.

She rattled some glasses in the kitchen, then lit another cigarette and waited.

Within a minute Jules and Daedalus came down from the workroom.

"Ah! Axelle," Daedalus said with a smile. "We've been waiting for you—there are some questions I have about the old Ville, and I knew if anyone could remember, it would be you."

"We just got here," said Jules. "Maybe five minutes ago. Now that you're here, we can get started."

"Okay. Just let me get something to drink," said Axelle. She poured some vermouth into a clean glass and looked at them. "Ready."

Mine Alone

In his dream, he still had a lifetime of potential. He was still looking forward to being a man, taller and broader, stronger. One day, not too far off, he would leave his father's house and have a house of his own. One day, when his father struck him, Richard would be big enough and strong enough to strike *him* down instead.

And he would be a man, a man that Cerise could have, if that sap Marcel hadn't managed to blackmail her into wifery by then. Another two years, Richard thought. He would be seventeen. Plenty old enough. In the meantime, he had to hold Cerise's interest. Which he seemed to be doing pretty well.

After months of chasing, where she'd laughed at him and called him a child, he thought he finally had her attention. She'd never been unkind, but she was older than he, and she had Marcel wooing her in his stolid, persistent way. Last month Richard had finally caught Cerise, caught her and held her against a tree, and kissed her till they were both breathless. They'd kissed twice more since then, longer and wilder each time. She wasn't laughing at him now.

Now when she looked at him, he saw his own hunger reflected in her eyes.

Then last week Richard had seen Marcel's patience finally break. After a circle he'd walked her home, while Richard followed in the darkness at a distance. After Cerise's mother and sister had gone in, Marcel had grabbed Cerise and kissed her. She'd squirmed gently out of his arms and held one hand against his cheek. "Dear Marcel," she'd said, and Richard had caught the words as if they were leaves borne to him by the wind. His hand had closed around the hilt of his hunting knife, but then Cerise had gone inside and Marcel had gone home.

She was old enough to marry Marcel, and Marcel was old enough to take her for his wife. Legally, Richard could marry at fifteen—he was of age, but he had no profession yet, no way of keeping a wife or providing for a family. It burned him.

But he and Cerise had lain in the meadow together, clinging together, kissing as if their lives depended on it. They couldn't stop themselves; they were wild with wanting, the air hot and damp on their skin. Richard surely had her attention now.

Then the dream changed and Richard was once again standing outside the general store, which was really just one front room of the Chevets' house. Marcel and Cerise were arguing. "You have to marry me," Marcel had said, his pale skin flushed and his fair, reddish hair burning in the sun. "You carry my child."

Richard's heart had squeezed as if in a vise, his breath knocked out of him.

"I'll not marry anyone," Cerise had hissed, while Madame Chevet had watched with fascination. "The child is mine alone!"

She'd grabbed her skirts and swept away, the market basket hanging heavy from her arm. Marcel had stood watching after her, grim determination on his face.

Several minutes had passed before Richard could breathe again, leaning against the building wall, out of sight. He felt like he was coming down with blood fever.

One truth was seared into his brain: Cerise had not admitted the child was Marcel's, but she hadn't denied it, either.

With a gasp Richard woke up, jackknifing into a sitting position. He was disoriented, looking around wildly. His heart was pounding and he was covered in a thin film of sweat that had nothing to do with the temperature.

Okay. He was in his room at Luc's. The bed felt clammy and he got up, sitting on the mattress edge as he fumbled for his cigarettes. He lit one with shaking hands and swallowed the hot smoke down. With his other hand he wiped the sweat off his forehead.

Sometimes he still hated Marcel so much his soul was black with it and it was hard to breathe.

Cerise. How could she still haunt his dreams after two centuries? God knew there had been hundreds of women since then. But Cerise had been the first. *Déesse,* how he'd loved her. He pictured her in his mind, then frowned—Cerise didn't have black hair. *Oh no.* Richard sucked in a breath so sharply it hurt. Cold sweat broke out on his skin and his hand trembled. Cerise with black hair was Clio. Or Thais.

He shook his head to clear the image out of his mind. He'd kissed Clio. He hadn't meant to, never planned to. The other day he'd just been rattling Luc's cage, teasing him about the twins just to mess with him. Last night Clio had been snide and unwelcoming—he could tell she didn't like him. He'd gotten a kick out of seeing her work like a dog. Even hot and sweaty and covered with dirt and grime, she was a beauty. They both were. Clio had been wearing that thin tank top and those itty-bitty shorts, and suddenly he'd wanted her. Which had been deeply disturbing and totally unwelcome.

But the way women dressed these days—Cerise had always been covered from neck to ankle. All the village women had. The naked female form had been a wondrous revelation that had almost made his head explode.

And here was Clio, on display. Those long, tan legs, slim, strong arms. Black hair pulled back into a messy ponytail. Green eyes snapping fire at him. He'd wanted her, wondered how those legs would feel wrapped around his waist, how tightly her arms could pull him to her. He still hadn't meant to kiss her, but then he had, and if she hadn't pushed him away, he wouldn't have stopped.

But she had. Which was good. He wished he'd never done it. He knew he'd never do it again. Never.

"Do you want to get some coffee?" Kevin asked. "Or something? Before you go home?"

I smiled at him, which made my face sting just a tiny bit. It was almost all healed. "That would be great." Just for a little while, I would play hooky from the massive house-cleaning job at home. Clio had said it was okay, and I was seizing the opportunity. These days I was so stiff and sore from all the cleanup work we were doing I could hardly move. I deserved a little break.

"Great." He started his car and pulled away from the curb outside of school. I watched him for a second, driving his little red Miata. "How about Botanika?"

"Uh, no," I said. No place where I might run into Luc. I had chanced it when I was with Clio and Racey but couldn't meet him like this, on my own. "How about that other one, on Magazine, off of Jefferson? What's its name?"

"Café de la Rue," said Kevin easily, turning off St. Charles Avenue toward the river. I had learned that no one used north, south, east, or west here when they gave directions. It was either toward or away from the river or toward or away from the lake. Since the river curled around the city like a shell, you had to know where you were, first, in relation to those two things before any directions made sense. In my mind, I thought of the lake as being north and the river as being east. But if you went east and crossed the river, then you were on the West Bank. I didn't get it, but I already knew that New Orleans had lots and lots of eccentricities that people accepted as normal and everyday and didn't question. It was kind of charming in a way, but it also made you feel crazy sometimes.

Café de la Rue was very different from Botanika. The people seemed to be mostly college students, and it had a slightly more formal, Old World feel, whereas Botanika was all about being funky and mystical and on the fringe.

We ordered our drinks and sat down at a little wooden table by the big sidewalk windows. There was a wide ledge there with potted plants and one of those little tabletop fountains that run on electricity. Its subdued trickling sound was soothing. All around us, people were working on laptops, alone or in pairs, some with headphones on. I drank my iced coffee, looking around, and I realized two things: one, I had drunk more coffee in the last month than I had in the seventeen years before then, and two, New Orleans has some of the best people-watching in the world.

"The whole long-lost-twin thing with Clio is so

weird," said Kevin, dumping sugar into his iced tea.

He had no idea. "Yeah, it really is. But it's great because I have a family again. Without my dad, I was just lost."

"That must have been really hard on you," Kevin said sympathetically. "My mom died when I was seven, and my dad got married again within a year. I still think it was because he didn't have any idea of what to do with me and my sister."

"I'm sorry," I said. "Do you get along with your stepmother?"

Kevin nodded. "Actually, I do. I mean, I remember it as being horrible at first, but she's been really good to me and my sister. Now she really seems like a mom."

"That's good," I said. "My dad never got married again, so it was always just me and him. Then he was gone. But now I have Clio and Petra, and things are starting to feel almost normal again."

"I'm glad." Kevin gave me a smile that went right from his eyes to my heart. He was just so sweet. Unfortunately, it was impossible not to compare him to Luc, and every time Luc seemed like the movie and Kevin like the TV show. Which was so awful and unfair of me. But Luc wasn't going to happen, and Kevin definitely could. I was determined to like him. And so far, it wasn't hard.

I don't know how long we'd sat there—Kevin was telling me stories about some of the teachers at school, and I was cracking up. He told me about getting cut off the football team after he broke his wrist, and he gave me the lowdown on some of the kids at school who I'd wondered about.

"Yeah, so she was on the debate team, and she was so stuck-up," he told me. "She just looked down on everyone, you know? And I worked my ass off—no one was more prepared. I mean, I had notes taped inside my shirt, I practiced on my whole family, I just got everything down cold, because I wanted to crush her."

"What happened?" I loved stories like this, especially because the girl he was talking about was in my French class and I couldn't stand her.

Kevin grinned, and I couldn't help laughing. "She never had a chance. Every single thing she came up with, I was totally ready. I just demolished her. If it had been anyone else, I would have felt really mean. But that girl so had it coming. I tore apart her arguments and hung her out to dry. She was near tears by the end."

"Oh, I wish I could have seen it," I said. "I would have loved it. What was your topic anyway?"

Kevin smiled wider. "Women on pro football teams," he said. "I was for."

I started laughing again and put my hand on his arm. Then suddenly I felt, literally felt, someone staring holes into the back of my head. Slowly I turned around.

Luc stood there with Richard. He looked better than when I had seen him at Axelle's—he had shaved and was wearing clean clothes—but his face was still drawn, almost haggard, and his eyes were filled with pain. And, uh, a bloodthirsty hatred.

And here I was, my hand on Kevin's arm, laughing up at him, our knees touching.

I was so, so thankful that it was here and now that I was running into Luc and not, say, when I was sobbing on Clio's shoulder or alone in a grocery store with a big zit or something.

Except, of course, that he was looking at me and Kevin like he was about to pull out an ax and come for us.

Kevin turned to see what I was looking at, and his eyes widened as he caught Luc's glare. "You know him?"

I shook my head. "Just a little," I said, thinking sadly how true that was. "He goes to the same church as . . . my grandmother."

Kevin looked back at me. "Well, he seems to have it bad for you." There was a question behind his words, but I couldn't go into it. I shrugged and shook my head.

Richard was grinning at me, the jerk, and I gave him a careless smile and wave. He'd come over twice to help with the windows, after all. Luc I ignored. I turned back to my coffee and took a long, slow sip, trying to get myself together. My heart was pounding, and my cheeks felt hot. I felt Kevin still looking at me, but I took another couple of moments to get a grip.

I swallowed hard, feeling like a wave had just rushed me off my feet at the beach. Oh God, I still wanted him so much. Loved him so much. I just *loved* him, wanted to be with him, to have him hold me. Wanted him to be mine, like he said he was, and for me to be his. My whole body was flooded with memories of Luc, how he felt, how he tasted. . . .

Of course, Clio had those same memories.

I swallowed again and looked up at Kevin with a bright smile. "This has been really great," I said. "Do you think—would you want to go to a movie sometime?"

Kevin looked happy, and I felt better. "Yeah, I'd like that a lot. Maybe this weekend? Should I call you?"

I wrote down Petra's number for him, and he put it in his pocket. I still felt awkward, still felt Luc's presence, and absently I reached over to trail my fingers in the little fountain on the window ledge. Then, out of nowhere, a rhyme popped into my head.

> Let me choose a path of light
> When my world is dark as night
> When my heart is so forlorn
> And love feels like a rose's thorn.
> I am sunlight, I am shade
> For love's sweet kiss my heart was made.
> But down that path my heartache lies
> Hidden in my lover's eyes.

It was a spell, I knew, but I had no idea where it came from or why. Or what it would do. It didn't exactly seem to have a point. *A spell.* Quickly I looked around, expecting the mirror over the counter to shatter or people's computers to start shooting sparks. But all was quiet.

"Uh," said Kevin.

I looked up at him to see him blinking dully at the table, then he started to slump sideways out of his chair.

"Kevin!" I got up quickly and grabbed his shoulders, easing him back into his chair. He felt slender and hard, like a statue, and he shook his head to clear it. "Are you okay?" I asked, trying to keep my voice down.

"Yeah," Kevin said, more strongly, and he blinked several times and sat up straighter. He rubbed his forehead with one hand and shook his head in bewilderment. "I don't know what happened," he said apologetically. "I just suddenly felt . . . weird. Sorry."

"No problem," I said. "I'm just sorry you feel bad. Do you think something's wrong? Are you getting sick?"

"I'm fine now," said Kevin, and he looked it. "I don't know what it was, but it's over." He smiled at me and I rubbed his shoulder.

"Why don't we just go?" I said, getting my purse. "I need to get home anyway—I told Clio I'd help her start dinner." It felt so great to know that someone was expecting me home, that I had someone I needed to check with. Someone cared about me.

"Okay." Kevin stood up, and he looked fine, no hint of dizziness or anything. As we were leaving the coffee shop, I couldn't resist glancing back quickly, just once, at Luc and Richard.

They were both watching me, and they both had odd expressions on their faces. Richard was looking at me with surprise and wariness, but Luc just seemed completely still and focused on me, as if he were an explorer and I were a new species and if he made any sound, I would run off.

Which I was going to do anyway.

I turned around and followed Kevin out of the café. Only I could pack so much emotion and anguish into getting an iced coffee.

You Yourself Want More Power

Daedalus looked at Axelle, lying on the couch, reading a magazine, and tried to keep the displeasure off his face.

He failed miserably.

She felt him watching her and looked up. "What?" she said, sounding irritated.

Well, he was irritated too. "There's work to be done. Why are you lying there reading that mindless drivel?"

"This is my house," she said flatly. "I do what I please."

"There are more useful things you could be doing," Daedalus said. "We're working toward a common cause. Your part used to be housing Thais until we were ready for her. What is your part now?"

Her eyes narrowed at him. "I bet you're dying to tell me."

"There are all sorts of things you could be doing for me!" Daedalus said. "I asked you to go to the little voodoo shop on Rampart Street, but you refused." He swung to look at Jules, standing in the kitchen. "And yes, you went, but you acted as if you were doing me a big favor. Do I have to remind you that we're all working together? I can't do everything myself."

"Yet you want to make all the decisions yourself," Axelle said coolly.

Daedalus was dumbfounded. Was she forgetting that he was the leader? He was always the leader. But he had always shared everything, given people important roles to play. "Did we or did we not agree that we were a team? That the three of us would get this thing done? I am trying to get this thing done." He looked down at Axelle. "What are you planning to contribute?"

Axelle looked at him, her eyes black and cold. "I'm not a servant girl, Daedalus. I'm not an *apprentice*. I agreed to be part of a team. I didn't agree to be your gofer, running about fetching you cold drinks while you run everything from your throne."

Quick anger rose in Daedalus, and with effort he damped it down. "You know," he said, almost to himself, "I'd forgotten it could be like this. But it's all coming back to me—the years I spent in Europe, traveling, learning. I met people, people who could contribute as much as I could. Useful people who understood the give-and-take of a working relationship."

"I wish you'd stayed there," Axelle muttered. She swung her legs off the sofa, leaned forward, and lit a cigarette.

"Now I find myself saddled with witches who have made no forward progress in a hundred years," he said bitingly. "It's unbearably frustrating. Don't you see? I'm doing this for all of us, not just me. I'm trying to satisfy *your* agenda. Not just mine."

Axelle stood up, facing him. "But it's your agenda that really matters, isn't it, Daedalus? You say that this is for everyone, but we don't really know that, do we? Face it—you're putting this together, this whole thing in motion, because you yourself want more power. That's what you want. If it works out for the rest of us, fine and dandy. If not, well, at least you got your power."

Daedalus was almost speechless. "How can you say that!" Axelle turned away from him and stalked toward the kitchen. He followed her. Jules was watching them both as he carved off slivers of Brie and layered them neatly on crackers.

"How can you say that!" Daedalus repeated angrily. "I've involved you from the beginning! I didn't have to bring you in on this, arrange to have you get Thais. I could have asked anyone else! I chose you because you're a valuable person to have on the team. I knew I could depend on you, trust you. Now Thais is under Petra's influence, and instead of throwing yourself into the thousand and one other things that need doing, you're sitting on your pretty ass, smoking cigarettes and reading magazines!" His voice ended in a roar, and Axelle turned, her beautiful, porcelain face flushed.

"I *am* valuable to you, Daedalus," she said in a tightly controlled voice. "But I don't think you understand how much. I'm willing to do my share if I'm an equal member of the team. I am not willing to be your errand girl, running to the store to get dried snakeskin or skullcap at your bidding. Get your own damned ingredients. For that matter, get your own food, your own alcohol, and your own car." She stepped closer to Daedalus, her chin raised to him. "Because right now, you're feeling a lot like a parasite."

Daedalus thought he would choke with rage. "A p-parasite!" he sputtered disbelievingly. "That's bloody ironic, coming from you! You, who's never lifted—"

"Hold it!" Jules had stepped forward, physically placing himself between Daedalus and Axelle. "Both of you! Stop it! You're tired and frustrated. You don't want to do this." Daedalus looked at him, so angry he could hardly speak. "Look," Jules went on, "the three of us are in this together. We need each other. You know how difficult it would be to pull this off if we three can't form the base for the others to lean on." He stepped back, looking from one to the other. "Let's take a break for the rest of the day. Tomorrow we'll meet back here, and we can calmly talk everything out, get everything on the table. Récolte is on Sunday—we're having a circle then. If the three of us can't present a united front then, this whole plan is doomed. Understand?"

Daedalus took a step back, forcing his hands to unclench. Jules might have something there. Best to let everyone calm down. No doubt they would be more reasonable tomorrow. He nodded stiffly and headed to the door, letting himself out.

Outside, the air seemed heavier and stiller than

usual. The scent of the river, two blocks away, was pervasive. Perhaps there would be a breeze up on the riverfront. He would walk up there and see, sit on a bench, watch the tugboats go by. That always soothed him.

Daedalus turned right, waiting for a horse and carriage to pass before he crossed the street. He hoped Axelle would come to her senses by tomorrow. If not, the whole thing would become unbearably unwieldy and difficult. And where were Marcel and Claire? They were ignoring his repeated summons. The two lone holdouts. His lips pressed together grimly. So far he had been playing nice with them, with Axelle and Jules, with everyone. But if things didn't fall into line soon, he would have to be more . . . persuasive. As for Marcel and Claire, it was definitely time for them to be called home by more forceful means.

Crying Was Pointless

Manon looked over at Sophie. She'd been sitting in front of her computer all morning, but for the last hour, she hadn't moved, hadn't typed anything. Her body was there, but her mind was somewhere else entirely.

Manon lifted her hair off her neck and stretched. Usually she could trust Sophie to tell her everything on her mind, share everything with her. She loved that about Sophie, how her face was so open, her emotions so transparent. But lately Sophie's face had been closed. She'd been distant. Ever since Manon had made her terrible admission.

Getting up, Manon came and hugged Sophie from behind. She leaned over so her head rested on Sophie's shoulder and put her arms around Sophie's waist. Sophie smiled and turned her head to Manon's. Manon curled one hand around Sophie's head and kissed her gently. She looked deeply into Sophie's artless brown eyes.

"What secret are you keeping from me?" she whispered.

"Nothing." Sophie shook her head.

"This is me," Manon persisted gently. "You can tell me anything."

"I don't want you to die," Sophie blurted, then looked away. "I don't want you to leave me."

Manon sighed and rested her head against Sophie's. At least Sophie was finally ready to talk about this. "I'm sorry if that hurts you," she said. "I don't want to leave you—I love you so much."

Sophie was still looking at her with wounded eyes. No one did wounded eyes better than Sophie.

"Sophie, you just don't understand what it's like, being me."

"I do understand," Sophie said, standing up. "I know it's frustrating—"

"It's so much worse than frustrating," Manon cut in. She gestured to herself, her slender, boyish body. "Look at me. I got frozen when I was thirteen years old. I don't even look like a *teenager*. And worse, I got frozen over two hundred years ago, when average heights were shorter. I'm four feet, six inches tall. I'll never look like a woman—it's almost impossible for me to feel like one."

"Manon, there are many grown women who are your height," Sophie said. "It's not as if you're a freak."

"Please," Manon scoffed. "We're all freaks. But Richard and I have it hardest. You know we do. I can't *stand* looking like a child. Women's rights—such as they are—have come a long way in the last hundred years, but I don't even have those. I can't buy property or wine or get into R-rated movies without you. I can't drive a damn car. I can hardly do anything without you. I'm so dependent on you, it makes me crazy."

"Is that what—?"

"Yet, thank the goddess I have you," Manon interrupted, pacing around the room. "Where would I be if I didn't have you? Can you even imagine? And what if you were a man? What if I loved you and you were a man? You would have been arrested a long time ago. There would have been no way for us to be together. People would think you were a pedophile. It's horrible. It turns our whole relationship into something twisted, something sick. Anyone who looked at us, you, a grown woman, me, looking this age, and knew we were lovers—it would be this horrible, unnatural crime in their eyes. I can't stand it! Not anymore."

"There are people who'd think it's sick and unnatural for us to be lovers even if they knew we were both way, way over twenty-one," Sophie pointed out.

Manon shook her head. "I'm doing it again," she said. "How many times have we had this exact same conversation? I rant about the same stuff, you say the same placating things—but don't you see? We'll be having this talk—I'll be having this problem—for the rest of my life. God, Sophie—it's just too long. Unbearably long." She held her cold can of soda against her forehead, trying not to cry. Crying was pointless. She'd been crying over this for more than two centuries and it hadn't gotten her anywhere. There was only one thing that would help.

Sophie came closer and put her hands on Manon's shoulders. "I know you're in pain. I see it, I see what you live with and go through. But you know I depend on you just as much as you depend on me. You know I would be just as lost without you. Can't I . . . don't I . . . aren't you happy enough with me to make it worthwhile to stay? I try to make you happy; I want you to be so happy with me that none of this will matter."

Manon heard tears in Sophie's voice. "You know I'm happy with you," she said quietly. "There's no one else who could make me happier. But how can I be part of a happy couple when my life is such a nightmare? I feel that way more all the time. What can I bring to you, to us, if I feel that way? In another decade, it will have made me stark raving *nuts*. And you'll be trapped with me, this embittered, crazy, desperately unhappy child/woman. How could you bear it? How could I bear doing that to you?"

Sophie was openly crying now. "Don't say that," she said. "How can you say that? I would love you no matter what! You look like a woman to *me*. You look like the only woman I'll ever want. But you want to leave me, to leave me alone forever!"

Manon put her arms around Sophie, feeling her sobs. She rested her head on Sophie's shoulder and held her tight, rocking her gently, stroking her long brown hair. "Forever is a long time to be alone," she said softly. "But it's a longer time to feel hopeless and wretched."

"No."

Thais turned to look at me. "What?"

"No," I said again, crossing my arms. "You may not go out on a fricking date wearing *that*. I mean, holy mother, what's wrong with you?"

Thais looked at herself again in the full-length mirror. "Why can't I wear this?"

"Because you look like a Girl Scout selling cookies." I shook my head in disgust. Identical, schmidentical. Clearly *I* had inherited every bit of fashion sense between us.

"What should I wear, then?" Thais sounded irritated, but I was already heading for my closet. Tonight she was going out on a real date with Kevin LaTour, and I'd be damned if I wasn't going to do everything in my power to make sure those two lovebirds hit it off. Given how much we looked alike, it was a nightmare for me to see myself dressed in a plain white T-shirt and a knee-length denim skirt. For a *date*.

Fortunately, my closet was chock-full of clothes that would make Thais look like the hottie I am.

Thais followed me into my room and sat on the bed. I glanced at her as I considered various options. We'd been doing laundry all week, sometimes washing things two and three times to get out the smell of smoke. "We're going for hot and available, but not slutty," I said, holding up a peasant blouse made of thin, crinkled cotton. I held it to my face and breathed in. Only the scent of detergent.

"Oh, good," Thais said dryly.

I looked at her. "Are you nervous?"

"I don't know. Not really, I guess. Kevin's really nice."

She didn't sound hyper with enthusiasm, and my chest tightened. The more she liked Kevin, the less Luc would mean to her. It wasn't that I wanted him for myself, that bastard, but something mean inside me just wanted Thais not to care about him anymore, as if that would somehow make him more mine. It was ugly, but it was there.

I tossed the peasant blouse over to the bed. "Put that on."

"How is this better than what I'm wearing?" Thais asked, pulling off her shirt.

"For one thing, it's just prettier, with all the embroidery. It looks girly, unlike your dockworker T-shirt. For another thing, all that elastic around the top makes guys feel like they can just tug it down."

Thais froze. "Ew!"

I shrugged. "You don't have to let 'em. But it puts the idea in their mind."

"And I would want that *why*?"

I sighed and shook my head, then found a black miniskirt that looked great with that top. "Just put this on and listen to the master."

Thais held it up. It came to mid-thigh. "And how do I sit down in this?"

"Let it ride up." Honestly, the girl was hopeless.

"How do I pick up something I drop?"

"Like this." I bent my knees, dropped into a crouch, then stood up. "Or let him get it."

She gave me a dirty look but put on the miniskirt. I switched out her plain silver hoops for some dangly earrings that almost brushed her shoulders.

"Your hair is fine, but we have fabulous eyes," I said, examining her face. "You should do more with them. And your skin is still a little pink, so we need to tone it down."

Ten minutes later, when Kevin rang the bell, Thais was ready. She looked fabulous, much more like me.

Nan and I hovered in the background as Thais opened the front door. I saw Kevin standing there, and Thais was right—he really was good-looking.

"*Whoa,*" I heard Kevin say, and then, "Uh, I mean, you look . . . really great."

Thais laughed, then waved goodbye to us and shut the door behind her.

"Did you want to meet him?" I asked Nan.

"I can meet him later," Nan said, heading into the workroom. "He seemed like a nice guy."

"And he's not a witch," I said, following her. "After

Luc, anyone else is simple." As soon as I said it, I winced and thought, *Crap*. I'd worked hard to not mention Luc's name—not to Racey, Nan, or Thais. I'd downplayed how I'd felt about Luc, how heartbroken and sick I was about it. I didn't want anyone to know. It was bad enough that *I* knew.

But of course Nan, as sharp as a shard of glass, caught it and turned to me.

"What do you need to tell me about Luc?" she asked gently.

"Nothing." Nor did I need to tell her that Richard had kissed me the other night. A fact I was still trying to suppress in my own memory. And I got to see *both* of them tomorrow night at the Récolte celebration. Goody.

I went to the cupboard and got out our four cups. We'd planned to work on scrying magick tonight since Thais would be out of the house and pathetic Clio didn't have a date with a normal, appropriate person who wasn't 250 years old.

Nan started to draw a circle on the floor with a thin line of sand flowing through her fingers. Chalk circles are good, all-purpose circles; circles drawn with salt have protective, purifying powers. Circles can be made out of almost anything—shells, rocks, gems, leaves, silk fibers—you name it. Today's circle of sand had powerful protective qualities because of what sand is made of: quartz, lime (in the form of ground-up, calcified shells), feldspar, mica, magnetite. They all had protective powers.

I set up the four cups and lit the incense and the

candle and then another pillar candle, a blue one, in the middle of the circle. Nan and I sat down, facing each other. It wasn't like it was before, before I knew she'd lied to me, kept my father from me. Just two months ago I had trusted her completely, put myself in her hands without question. Now I knew that I couldn't. I wondered if it would interfere with our magick, our connection.

I looked up to see her watching me, as if she knew what I was thinking. With a small, sad smile, she took my hands, then closed her eyes.

Eventually Nan started singing, and I joined in with my own song when I felt ready. We each watched the candle flame between us, and soon I had become part of it. I saw the almost-clear base of fire, faintly tinged with blue, that seemed to hover at the bottom of the wick. Then the orange parabola that rose above it, burning steadily. Above that, the peak of white and yellow, swaying, undulating, burning like life itself. The essence of fire became bigger than the candle flame, as though this small mote had broken off a raging inferno and somehow landed here. I could feel its appetite, its eagerness to consume. It seemed so pure, so above considerations of good or bad. It just *was* itself, with neither pride nor remorse.

I wanted to be fire.

Then, as I gazed dreamily at it, my vision opened up to see a campfire on the ground. An iron pot was boiling above it, supported on a trestle. I looked around and saw a village. A narrow road, covered with crushed oyster shells, wound through an uneven line of wooden houses. It looked like a movie set, and I walked down the road, curious. A pig ran past, squealing, followed by two small boys with sticks. Loose chickens pecked in the dirt by the side of the road. I smelled wood smoke.

One smaller house stood a little ways off the road. It was painted yellow and had flowers and herbs growing in the yard. It felt like a place I knew, and I walked toward it. The front door was open, and a cat ran out of it, followed by a woman with light brown hair, almost blond. It was Nan, a much younger Nan, holding a toddler on her hip. Her lips were pressed tightly together and she seemed distracted.

Then a man came out of the house, holding a valise made of carpet. It was the same man we'd seen arguing with Nan in our vision. He was tall and handsome, with black hair. He had my birthmark on one cheek, but his skin was tanned so darkly you could hardly see it. He said something to Nan, and she shook her head angrily, not looking at him. He let out a breath, threw up his hands, and walked away from them. A horse was tethered nearby and he got on it, then rode off into the distance out of sight.

The scene changed abruptly, and Nan was much older, as old as she looked now. She was in a small room, standing by a narrow bed. Her forehead was damp with sweat and she looked tired. A girl I recognized as Sophie stepped forward and handed her a basin of steaming water and a towel. A young woman was on the bed, not the girl from the rainy night who died, but someone different. She had brown hair, brown eyes, and our birthmark but still somehow looked like a young Nan.

She was in labor, and Nan was helping. The baby was born, and Nan lifted it and tied the cord with string. Sophie smiled happily and took the baby in a white cloth. Then Nan looked alarmed and leaned over the girl in the bed, grabbing her hand. The girl's face was pleased and relaxed, her eyes staring blankly at the ceiling. She was dead. I felt Nan's grief, her anger, a huge sense of despair. In another scene I saw Nan fill out the death certificate. The girl's name had been Béatriz Rousseau. The year was 1818.

The baby had had a birthmark too. That birthmark had been handed down in our family for generations, as though we were marked for death even before we had lived.

I didn't want to see anymore and felt myself closing off. I was half aware of sitting on the workroom floor, and then I felt Nan's warm hands slowly pulling themselves out of mine. She drew away and left me, clearly meaning for me to continue practicing my skills.

I didn't know what to scry for. I didn't want to see any more of the past, see how generations before me had died, one after another, like dominos, in childbirth. Like my mother. I had the sudden realization that I myself would die like that if I had a child. I would die. I'd never thought about children, didn't even know if I wanted any. If Luc and I had stayed together somehow, would I have wanted to have his child? A gulf of longing and emptiness rose inside me, thinking of it.

I shook my head. This wasn't scrying. I wasn't concentrating. I could think about all this later.

Luc. God, Luc. Would I ever not miss him? Not want him?

Then he was right in front of me; I was scrying him in the flame. I hadn't meant to—my longing had opened this door. But now that I was here, I didn't close it. I hadn't seen him in days and my eyes feasted on him, as if I could consume him just by looking.

Luc was in a dark, swampy, woodsy place. He was kneeling on the ground, surrounded by crystals and hunks of salt rock. Before him was a broad, shallow bowl of water. He was working magick.

He blinked and looked up, right into my eyes.

I drew in a startled breath and winked out my vision, dousing the candle. I swallowed and opened my circle quickly, my heart pounding. I was ashamed of spying on him, yet everything in me was singing with joy at seeing him again, just for a moment.

I put away our tools and swept up the circle. I heard Nan in the kitchen and hoped she wasn't doing any of the cleanup, which would only make me feel worse. Though of course I would be happy to do less.

I had seen Luc, and he'd been working magick. For what? I would have given anything to know what he'd been doing. What if the two of us made magick together, joining our hearts and minds, losing ourselves in a magickal place where power and life were all around us? It would be heaven, as close as I would ever get to heaven, since our religion didn't have a heaven or a hell.

Luc loved Thais. He'd used me and lied to me and made me love him. I hated him for it—yet pathetically, I admitted only to myself that I still loved him despite everything. And I would be seeing him tomorrow night.

"So *Ponchartrain* is a Native American word, right?" I asked Kevin. We were walking along the levee at the lakefront, hoping to catch any kind of breeze. We'd gone to a movie, which I could already hardly remember, but it had been mildly funny and not too bad.

"Yeah," Kevin said, taking my hand. "Look up ahead. There's a neat fountain I want to show you."

As we headed down the sidewalk, I began to catch on to the fact that the lakefront was a major parking and make-out spot. There were also tons of people just standing around their cars, talking, drinking beer. Other cars drove past and called to them or razzed them. It was a whole scene, and we hadn't had anything like it in Welsford.

I was liking Kevin more the better I knew him. It wasn't an overwhelming, joyous, desperate thing, like it had been with Luc, but it was pleasant and nice. Which was a welcome change.

"Oh my gosh," I said as we came closer to the fountain.

"It's called the Mardi Gras fountain," Kevin said.

"It was made back in 1962, and just last year it didn't work and was all broken. But they've restored it. It's cool."

It was an enormous fountain surrounded by a black wrought-iron fence. Around the concrete base was a ring of tiled plaques, and we walked closer to see them.

"Each one is for a different Mardi Gras krewe," Kevin explained. "Some of them don't exist anymore, and the new ones aren't shown. But a lot of them are still around."

We walked slowly around the fountain, reading the plaques. The names of the krewes were weird and funny: Momus, Comus, Zulu, Osiris, Rex. The fountain itself shot maybe twenty feet into the air, with rings of jets that played at different times and heights to make it seem patternless. Plus lights set into the bottom changed the color of the water itself from purple and green and gold, to just one shade, to red and blue and all sorts of combinations.

It was bizarre, overdone, and gaudy yet beautiful and strong. Very New Orleans.

"This is awesome," I said sincerely. "I love this. Thanks for showing it to me."

Kevin smiled down at me. "It's cool, isn't it? My folks used to take me here when I was little."

"And now you bring girls here," I teased him.

"Uh, a few." He grinned.

"Are they supposed to be doing that?" I pointed to some people who had climbed over the fence and were actually playing and splashing in the fountain.

Kevin shrugged. "No. But people always do. Sometimes people soap it too. There are fountains all over the city, and people always play in them. It's too hot to not take advantage of a chance to cool off."

"You're right about that." Here it was, practically October, ten o'clock at night, and it was probably still in the high eighties. I reached back and lifted my hair off my neck to let the breeze get to it. Leaning over, Kevin blew softly on my neck to cool me off.

It was really intimate and really sweet. I looked into his green eyes, a more olive shade than mine, and wondered if he was going to kiss me. But he drew back and gestured to the fountain.

"Wanna join them?"

"Yeah!" We climbed easily over the low fence, and I kicked off my sandals, the only part of my outfit that Clio had approved of. Kevin took off his Tevas, then led me over the shallow rim of the fountain.

Immediately the smaller jets shot up, raining down on us. People around us were playing and laughing, pretending to really splash each other. When we got wet, I gave a little shriek, but Kevin was laughing, and he took my hand and pulled me away from a group that was getting too raucous.

The water was almost cool, and it swirled around my legs. "This feels great," I said, wading, looking at my bare feet lit up by the fountain lights.

"And your skirt's so short you don't have to worry about it getting wet," Kevin said.

Quickly I looked at him and saw a gentle, teasing expression on his face. He made me feel so comfortable, as if I could totally trust him. "You noticed it, did you?" I said.

"Oh, *yeah*."

I laughed, and then my foot hit something and I almost lost my balance. Kevin grabbed me, and I saw that I'd run into a little faucet handle set into the fountain floor.

"Thanks," I said, then realized he hadn't let me go. He looked at me, not smiling, and I thought, *Here we go*, and caught my breath. Slowly Kevin lowered his head, giving me time to escape, but I didn't and met his lips with mine, actually kissing someone else besides Luc, which I thought I'd never do again for the rest of my life.

Kevin was a good kisser. He was much more sure of himself than Chad Woolcott had been, and there was none of the deep, heavy urgency that Luc's kisses had ignited. Instead it was sweet and exploring, not tentative. I kissed him back, and pathetically, I was glad that Luc wouldn't see this. Then I was so mad that I'd even had that thought, and I went up on my toes and wrapped my arms around Kevin's neck. It didn't seem to matter that we were out in public, that tons of people could see us.

At that moment, it was as if someone flicked a switch and turned off the moonlight. Despite the overhead lights around the fountain and the water lights themselves, the area still somehow seemed draped in sudden darkness. A chilly breeze made goose bumps rise on my arms, and I pulled back from Kevin and looked at the sky. Huge, dark thunderclouds were rolling in off the lake, blocking the moon and stars.

Suddenly everything was washed out, so brightly lit with lightning that all color was leached out of my sight, as if an enormous camera flash had gone off.

"Move!" Kevin said, starting to pull me to get out of the fountain. Everyone else was scrambling to get out, and then a huge *boom!* of thunder seemed to shake the earth itself. I was hurrying through the knee-deep water, but about a foot from the edge I had a shocking premonition of death, danger, dying. Without a moment to think, I yanked my hand out of Kevin's and threw my arms into the air. Closing my eyes, I cried out the strongest protection spell Petra had taught me, hoping I had memorized the syllables correctly. Then I said, "Goddess, hear me! I call on earth, water, fire, and air! Protect us!"

In the next millisecond, an enormous bolt of lightning snaked down from the sky, making my hair fly up with electricity. I smelled something burning, and then the lightning hit the water we were standing in. My whole body tingled, and the fountain's lights all around us burst, with glass and sparks flying everywhere. But Kevin and I were protected, as if we were in a bubble that slowed time down and absorbed the enormous voltage of the lightning bolt. I whirled in slow motion and saw Kevin, looking stunned, reaching for me. Oh goddess, my magick had worked! For once, it had worked properly! Ecstatic joy flooded me, and I raised my face to the sky and laughed. In the next fraction of a second, I saw Luc's face, right in front of me, his eyes wide and startled, alarm making him still. But my magick had worked and now flowed out of me seamlessly, and I was part of the world again.

Then Kevin started to fall, the moment seemed to pop, and suddenly I was back in the now, hearing scared cries, the fountain's silence, the distant honking of cars. I lunged forward, almost slipping, and caught Kevin. He was heavy, and the best I could do was sink down against the fountain ledge, propping him against me. Had my spell protected only me? I was suddenly terrified. We'd been standing in water that lightning struck—we should have been killed. But was Kevin more hurt than I was?

"Kevin! Kevin!" I said, holding him in my arms. A man ran over and helped me get him out of the fountain. Kevin shook his head and blinked, looking up at me.

"My God!" said the man. "Never seen anything like it! You two should be dead!"

"Are you okay?" I asked Kevin worriedly, keeping my arms around him.

"Yeah," he said slowly. "What happened?"

"We got hit by lightning, sort of," I said with a nervous laugh.

"Y'all better get out of here before you get hit again," said the man as heavy rain began to fall. "Storm looks bad."

"Can you walk? Are you okay?" I asked again.

He nodded and got to his feet. He rubbed his forehead with one hand, looking confused. "I'm okay," he said. "I just don't remember what happened." He seemed more himself, and he took my hand. "Let's get to the car—we're getting soaked."

Together we ran back to where he had parked the little Miata. Inside I felt cold, either from the temperature drop or a delayed reaction. I had made magick. I had saved us. It was exhilarating. And scary. And I had seen Luc, right when my spell had occurred. Why? What did that mean? Had he . . . been part of it somehow?

"You're shaking," said Kevin.

"I am? Oh. Yeah, I am."

He reached into the minuscule backseat and pulled out a soft cotton throw. It was big enough to wrap around both of us, even over the stick shift, and I immediately felt better.

"Are you okay?" I asked for the third time. "Should we go to a doctor?"

"My dad's a doctor," he said, "but actually, I feel okay. A little shook up, maybe, but fine. So lightning hit the actual water?"

I nodded. "It broke all the lights. It was pretty scary. I felt like I'd stuck my finger in a light socket."

He shook his head, trying to figure it out. "It should have killed us—a fountain that small, a direct hit. I don't know why it didn't."

I shrugged, wide-eyed, realizing suddenly that Kevin hadn't heard my spell. "Just lucky, I guess."

"Yeah," he said, not sounding convinced. The rain was pouring down now, with more lightning and huge, rolling booms of thunder, but I felt cozy and safe inside the small dark car. Kevin seemed normal again at last, and he started the engine and took me home.

At Petra's, I asked if he wanted to come in and dry off, but he shook his head.

"Think I'll just go home. But . . . do you want to go out with me again? If I promise not to put you in death-defying situations?" He actually sounded uncertain, and I laughed.

In answer I reached up and put my arms around him, and smiling, he kissed me. He felt warm and smooth and very comforting, and we kissed for a long time, standing there on the porch. Then I felt Clio coming toward the front door, and I broke away.

"I better go in," I said. The rain had stopped while we were kissing, and now the world was dripping wetly.

"Okay. I'll call you." He let me go reluctantly, and I watched him get back into his car and drive away.

I couldn't get one thought out of my brain: I had made magick. And it had worked.

Endless, Pain-Edged Days

Luc wiped the cold sweat from his brow. He sat back on his heels, breathing hard, as if he'd been running. *Get a grip.* The intense darkness surrounded him, and he blew out the candles he'd been using to make the darkness more complete. All around him he could hear night sounds—animals foraging or stalking, insects humming, the rustling of owls as they flew through the trees.

God. Thais. The endless, pain-edged days were making him literally sick—he'd lost weight, couldn't sleep, could hardly eat. He'd been drinking most of his meals ever since she'd ripped him out of her life.

He felt like he'd been flayed alive and Thais was the balm that would heal everything, make him whole again. He missed her solemn face, her quick laugh, the way she touched him. She'd been shy and a little scared, yet she'd never held back from him. She'd given everything he'd asked for, given it freely and with all her strength.

He'd seen her tonight, scrying. She'd been wrapped around that kid, kissing him, their mouths open, drinking from each other. It twisted in Luc's gut like an *athème*. It had been unbearable.

His heart was going to explode. Angrily he smashed the bowl of water aside, then picked it up and brought it down hard on the salt chunks he'd been using. The heavy stone bowl smashed them into powder, and feeling rage wash over him, Luc raised the bowl again and slammed it down, twice, three times. The third time the bowl itself broke, and Luc stared at the shards in disbelief.

This was his main tool, the bowl his mother had used and her mother before that. It was incredibly old and had a carved border of *plumes* around the top. His grandfather's element had been air, his grandmother's water, and the bowl had symbolized their joined powers. He'd always used it in his magick, used it to scry, to hold water or fire. Now he'd broken it, and it could never be repaired. One of the biggest shards had an almost complete *plume*, a feather, on it. He picked it up and stroked the cool stone against his cheek.

Remorse doused his rage. Dropping his head into his hands, he tried to slow his breathing, cool his blood. The bowl was broken forever, like his relationship with the one person he'd actually loved over the last two hundred years.

Sighing, Luc stripped off his shirt and walked over to the narrow river running twenty feet away. The cold water was clear and red-tinged. He dunked his shirt into it and wrung it out, then squeezed it over his face and shoulders. It felt incredible. Standing up, he pushed off his jeans and then, naked, walked out into the river. It was shallow, barely up to his waist, and cool against his hot skin. He dunked under, getting his hair wet and pushing it out of his eyes. He leaned back, looking at the sky. Tall trees on either side of the river left only a narrow channel of dark sky above him. Sinking down till the water was up to his shoulders, Luc watched the stars and thought.

He wanted Thais. Neither twin wanted him. Or . . . was that really true? It always came back to the plan. The plan called for his being with one of them. It didn't matter which one. And it had to happen soon, if it was going to work at all.

"What's up?" Clio said, looking around the front door at me. Then she really saw me. "Whoa. Guess you got caught in the rain. You look like you got dragged through a hedge backward."

I made a face and followed her into the house. "Thanks." I felt cold and damp and chilled all the way through.

"Thais?" said Petra, running into the room, her brow furrowed in worry. "Are you all right? A while ago I felt—I don't know. I just felt you somehow." She looked me up and down, and her frown deepened. "You're all wet."

"Yeah. It's been kind of a full night. Let me put on something dry, okay?"

"I'll make something hot to drink," said Petra, watching me as I climbed the stairs. "But you're sure you're okay?"

I nodded. "Yeah, pretty okay. Considering I got hit by lightning."

"Tell me again." Petra looked at me seriously across the kitchen table.

I took another sip of hot chocolate, surprised it wasn't some herbal magickal anti-damp-and-wet concoction.

"We went to the Mardi Gras fountain, by the lake," I said again. I'd already told them once, but I guess Petra was hankering for any juicy details I'd missed. "A bunch of people were playing in it, so we got in too. And then, completely out of nowhere, it was storm city. There was lightning and everyone was yelling to get out of the fountain. Do we have any cookies?"

Clio tilted her head toward the pantry, and I went and got the package of cookies.

"So everyone was scrambling to get out of the fountain," I went on, trying not to spit crumbs. "We were rushing to the side, but then I suddenly felt that we were about to get hit by lightning. So I just shouted out that protection spell you taught me, not even sure I was remembering it correctly. And I called on earth, water, fire, and air to protect us. And it was like we were in a little bubble, and the lightning hit the water and made my hair stand on end, practically. Then the bubble popped, and it was all over, and Kevin fainted."

Petra didn't say anything, thinking it through. She looked very solemn, her long fingers wrapped around her mug. I ate another cookie.

"It's lucky he only fainted," said Clio. "You guys both should have been killed."

"That's what some guy said at the fountain," I said. "But I mean, I think my magick actually worked somehow. It felt . . . smooth. Usually it feels like something extra, like a cloak that I'm shrugging off or pushing off, you know? But this felt so . . . light and easy, but really strong and smooth. It's hard to describe. It felt right, like . . . like I was a flower and the magick was a scent. Part of me, but going out into the world. But I made it." I realized how stupid that sounded and shook my head, embarrassed. And still Petra was looking at me. "Isn't this good? Isn't this what it's supposed to be? I didn't blow anything up."

"It's good," said Petra.

"I know what you mean," Clio said, surprising me, and Petra nodded.

"That's what it's supposed to feel like," she said. "It hasn't felt like that before?"

"No, not really," I said. Then I remembered something. "Oh, one other time. I was at the coffee shop with Kevin, and all of a sudden a little rhyme came into my mind. I said it, and it felt like that, smooth and easy and part of me, but going out."

Petra frowned. "What were you doing in the coffee shop?"

"Um, just getting coffee?"

She smiled briefly and shook her head. "No, I meant, what exactly were you doing at the exact moment the rhyme came to you?"

"You were with Kevin that time too," said Clio. "Like he helps your magick somehow. Interesting."

"Was there a tea light on the table? Were you playing with it?" Petra asked.

I thought. "No. Oh, but you know, there was a little

electric fountain in the window, a little tabletop one. I remember I was playing with it, dipping my fingers in it."

"Hmm." Petra sat back, looking both satisfied and thoughtful at the same time.

"What?" I asked.

"I think I understand something now, something I didn't see before," said Petra. "I'm surprised, but of course now it makes perfect sense."

"What?" I said again.

"Yeah, *what?*" said Clio.

"Your element," said Petra. "We've assumed that it was fire because Clio's is, and actually mine is too. But it seems clear now—that protection spell worked so well, and felt so right, because you were surrounded by your true element—water."

Clio and I just sat there, speechless for a moment. Finally I found my voice.

"Water! But why would water be my element?"

"It's the opposite of fire," said Petra. "You two are *mirrors* of each other, not clones."

"That explains your fashion sense," Clio said brightly, and I kicked her. "Ow!"

"Huh. Water." I was having trouble taking it in. I hadn't been doing magick long, but what I'd done had been focused around fire. "But what does this mean?"

"It's probably why the magick you've been trying to make has backfired," said Petra. "And why it's felt hard and unnatural."

"I thought it was just because making magick *is* hard and unnatural," I said.

Petra smiled bigger. "Is that still what you think?"

I thought back to when I'd cried out the protection spell, how exhilarated I'd felt, how simple everything had seemed. In that one moment, it was as if the whole world had fallen into place, and everything had made sense, if only for a second. My magick had worked perfectly, flowing seamlessly out from me into the world. Tears came to my eyes as I remembered that beautiful, ecstatic feeling.

"No." I smiled. Now I knew. My element was water. If I worked with my true element, magick felt like nothing else in the world, like perfection. And it was within my grasp.

Petra reached across the table and took my hand in hers, lightly patting it. "Water," she murmured, looking at me. "I never would have thought. . . ."

"We're doing what now?" Thais asked. "Today is what?"

"Récolte," I said. I straightened from where I was dribbling seed on the ground in a pattern. The backyard still looked like a demilitarized zone, with scorched plants, cracked flowerpots, and leftover building material from where some of the weatherboards had been replaced. We were due to go to our circle pretty soon—because it had to be outside, it was being held over in Covington, across the lake. It would take about forty minutes to get there.

"The autumn equinox," Nan said. "In our religion there are eight *jours sacrés*. Eight holy days, remember, I told you about them? The four main ones and four minor ones?"

Thais looked embarrassed. "I don't remember them too well."

"Well, Récolte is one of the minor ones," Nan said. "It's the second of three traditional harvest festivals, and it takes place on the autumn equinox every year."

"Today the length of the night and the day are

exactly the same," I explained. "All the days after this will be shorter, and the nights longer, until spring. It's sort of about getting the harvest in, getting ready for winter."

"So what's with the seeds?" Thais asked.

"I'm making the rune *seige* with seeds," I said, kneeling down to finish it. "The rune for the sun. Today the sun is going underground for winter, and we'll see him again in the spring."

"Uh-huh." Thais sounded unconvinced.

"You'll understand more at the circle," Nan said, brushing off her hands. She glanced at her watch. "Actually, we better get moving. We need to be there before dusk."

Covington was directly across the lake, so we took the causeway, the longest bridge in the world, to get there.

"Why do we have to do the circle outside?" Thais looked out her window. We were at the middle part of the causeway, where you couldn't see land on either side—only water all around. Little whitecaps kicked up here and there, and gulls circled overhead, occasionally dipping down to snatch a fish.

"Because it's about celebrating nature," Nan said, keeping her eyes on the road. "It's about thanking the earth for the bounty we've harvested and honoring her as a life giver. After the circle, we'll have a feast, with lots of fresh-baked breads and wine and seed cakes."

"You usually do this with your other coven?" Thais asked.

Nan nodded. "Yes. But they understand that I need to do some things with the Treize right now. I need to find out more about what they're gathering for and find out how they all feel about it."

"You know what they've gathered for," I said from the backseat. "They want to do the rite that'll find their fountain of youth again and get them even more power."

"Yes." Nan met my eyes in the rearview mirror. "But I think there are other layers to what's going on. I want you two to be extra careful and keep your eyes open. Don't wander off, okay?"

"Okay," I said, and Thais nodded, looking less than thrilled.

I was concerned myself: tonight I would see Luc in person for the first time since the night I'd kicked him out of the house. So much had happened since then. I smoothed my thin linen *bouvre* over my knees. Thais had started off wearing a blue T-shirt and a jeans skirt, but Nan had asked her to borrow a *bouvre* from me. "A what?" she'd asked, and Nan had explained that usually at circles and always on holidays, witches wore the long, loose gown. Nan's was almost always a sky blue silk, but she had a gold one for the harvest festivals. I'd lent Thais a flowy, thin cotton one in a russet that looked pretty with our coloring. It had a gathered neck and loose sleeves that wouldn't be too hot. I hadn't been able to get her out of her Tevas.

I, on the other hand, was stretching the definition of *bouvre*. Yes, it was long and a little loose and flowy, but it was also a halter top and made out of scarlet linen. Racey always said it looked like it came from "Tarts R Us," but I loved it and knew I looked incredibly hot in it. And I needed to look incredibly hot tonight. I wanted Luc to see exactly what he had lost. Maybe he thought he loved Thais, but he'd felt something for me. Maybe not love, maybe only desire, but something, and I wanted to rub it in.

"It will be interesting, seeing if you feel this circle any differently now that you know your true element," Nan went on to Thais.

"Yeah. I want to try to work some magick again, like with Clio," she said.

"That's fine, but I'd like you to make sure I'm around when you do," said Nan.

"Why?" Thais looked surprised, but just then Nan reached the end of the causeway. She took the first left, following a small road that wound around the lake.

She never did answer.

Five minutes later Nan turned and drove through an open wooden gate marked Private Property.

"This belongs to one of my friends," she explained, heading down a winding, overgrown road. "I like being on familiar territory. We've had circles here before."

I'd never been here, so I wasn't sure what circles she was talking about. I knew she and about five other women met sometimes to deepen their study of magick—maybe that had been it.

There was no visible house, but we saw several other

cars under a row of live oaks, and Nan pulled up next to one. "Can you two get our things from the trunk? I'd like to find Ouida," she said, turning off the engine.

"Sure," said Thais, and Nan got out, leaving us in the car.

"How do you feel?" I asked.

Thais turned around to look at me. "Nervous. I don't want to see him."

I liked how we were so often in tune with what the other was thinking. One of our twin things. Racey and I were like that, but Thais and I didn't even really know each other that well yet.

"I know," I said. "But I also want to show him that I'm perfectly fine and not all torn up, you know? I want to look totally normal, like I don't care. Like it didn't affect me."

Thais nodded. "It's going to be hard."

"Yeah." I was also going to face Richard. Every time I remembered that I'd let him kiss me, I felt weird all over again.

"Plus, you know, the whole someone's-trying-to-kill-us thing," said Thais, leaning her head against her window. "Probably someone here."

I sighed. "Well, we can't stay in the car all night. The circle has to start right before dusk. They'll come get us in a minute."

Thais sighed too, sounding exactly like me. "Okay. Let's go."

Right through the trees was a large natural clearing. Wild grass grew halfway to my knees. At one end, tables had been set up, and several members of the Treize were there, putting out platters and glasses.

"I'm not eating or drinking anything until I see someone else try it first," Thais muttered as we brought Nan's bread over.

I smiled grimly and nodded. Nan was standing next to Ouida. I saw Sophie and the little-girl-looking witch, Manon, standing by themselves talking, not far away. Sophie was always so solemn—it made her seem much older than she looked.

Oh, right. God, the whole immortal thing was still really hard to deal with.

"Here's the quinoa salad," said Thais, placing it on the table.

"Thanks," said Nan.

"And bread." I put it on a wooden cutting board that had already been set out.

"How have you two been?" Ouida asked sympathetically.

"Okay," I said. "Better, now that Nan's back."

"I bet. Has anything else dangerous happened?"

"You mean, besides us setting the house on fire?" I said dryly. "No. Oh, except Thais got hit by lightning."

"I wanted to tell you about that," Nan said as Ouida's eyes widened. She started to tell the story about Thais's true element.

"Did you bring the wine?" I asked Thais, looking at the table.

"No—there's already some here."

"Nan brought some too. You know, I think it's in

the backseat." I hoped Thais would offer to get it, but she didn't, so I headed back to the car myself. It was within full view of where we were, fortunately.

I was headfirst into the car's backseat when I suddenly felt someone watching me. I grabbed Nan's two bottles of wine and stood up quickly, thinking, *Luc.*

But it was Richard who leaned against the next car, Richard who was watching me with those dark brown eyes. "Hello," he said. "Nice *bouvre.*" He was wearing beat-up green fatigue pants and a white T-shirt with the sleeves ripped off.

"Do any of your shirts have sleeves?" I asked.

He gave me a little grin. "In the winter." He grabbed the hem of his shirt and pulled it over his head so he was naked from the waist up. I saw he had another thorny tribal tattoo on his smooth chest. Then he leaned through an open car window and pulled out his own *bouvre,* which was raw silk, streaky brown and gold, like his hair. He pulled it on and it settled lovingly around him. Then, as if I wasn't even there, he reached under it and I heard his pants unsnap. Immediately I turned and started walking away.

"Wait," he said.

I turned to him, glad I was wearing two-inch wedge espadrilles. He was only an inch or two taller than me now. I stood there stone-faced as he kicked out of his fatigues and picked them up off the ground.

"If you're trying to make me go mad with lust, you're failing," I said in a bored tone.

He gave me a slight grin and pushed his clothes

into the car. Then out came the ever-present cigarette, which he lit.

"I have to go," I said impatiently.

He pulled on the cigarette, his head down, as if he was thinking. Then he looked up at me again and blew the smoke out of his nose, like a dragon.

"I wanted to say I'm sorry," he said, and I blinked in surprise.

"For what?"

"Kissing you. The other night."

I looked at him suspiciously, but there was no irony in his eyes, no second meaning behind his words. I shrugged and shook my head, not knowing what to say.

"I didn't mean to," he went on. "I won't do it again."

He gave me a little smile, almost sad, then turned and walked to the clearing. I heard Daedalus call his name. I stood there frozen, pulling in a shallow, silent breath. Swallowing hard, I realized I felt shaken, which was ridiculous. There was absolutely no reason why I would feel upset or even, goddess, hurt, just because Richard hadn't meant his kiss.

It didn't matter to me at all.

"Can I have some wine?" I asked Nan breathlessly when I got back.

She poured me half a glass. "That has to last you all night."

"Okay." She moved off, now talking to Axelle, Jules, and Ouida. I took a sip, feeling its warmth as it went down, and realized wine was the last thing I wanted right now. I put it down.

"Do we have any lemonade?" I asked Thais. "Or water? Iced tea?"

"Tea. Here." She handed me a glass already poured. "So, the wine—it doesn't matter that you're underage?"

I thought about it. "Well, I'm not driving, and it's just half a glass. You know, it's just tradition. Family tradition. French families start giving their children a tiny bit of wine at dinner when they're just little kids. I mean, I'm not hanging out at the 7-Eleven, swilling beer."

Thais nodded, processing. "You know, these boo-thingies are really comfortable," she said. "And it even looks okay on the male people."

I drank almost half the tea right away. "That's better. Yeah, they're like kilts," I agreed. "On the right guy, they can even be really sexy." Then I winced. We both knew who we'd be seeing in a *bouvre* tonight.

Besides Richard, that is. I kept my back to the clearing, not wanting to see him again. I hadn't told Thais about his kissing me, hadn't even told Racey. Usually I told Racey everything, so I didn't know why I had kept it to myself.

I felt Thais stiffen by my side and turned. She was staring at me, her eyes wide and leaf green. Then I felt Luc's presence getting nearer. I reached out one hand and patted her arm, and she tried to smile.

We turned to look at him at the same time.

"Loser," I said coolly in greeting.

Luc's beautiful dark blue eyes looked into mine, as if he could see my soul. Goddess, what was it with me and guys? A guy had never knocked me off balance before in my life, yet Luc and now even Richard seemed to do it as easily as breathing.

Luc nodded. "Yes. I have lost," he said, and just hearing his voice sent shivers down my spine. Instantly my body woke up, every nerve ending coming to life, remembering his touch, his kisses, the way he felt when we were lying together.

Thais wasn't even looking at him, just staring at the ground, her body as stiff as a statue. I felt a second of irritation with her—I wanted her to have the Clio coolness, Clio strength. I didn't want her to seem this young, this vulnerable. It was almost like it made *me* look weak.

"How's your boyfriend?" Luc asked her, his voice chilly.

She looked up then, and I saw a spark in her eyes that surprised me. "He's fine," she said evenly, and I almost smiled. "Maybe I'll see him later tonight." She sounded distant, uninterested, and I was proud of her.

Luc's face flushed and his eyes narrowed. He wasn't going to win any awards for his ability to conceal emotion. My jaw clenched. Emotion he felt for my *sister*. "We won't be done till late," he said, his voice tight.

Thais shrugged casually and took a sip of tea. "That's okay."

"It didn't take you long," he said, sounding angry.

Thais shrugged again. I saw a faint pink tinge on her neck—she was about to flush. She wasn't as unaffected by Luc as she was pretending. She put her glass down and walked away without another word, leaving me and Luc alone.

"Why don't you run after her?" I asked snidely. I shook my hair back over my shoulders, feeling anger erupting inside my chest. "She's the one you care about."

Luc turned to face me. I thought he would snap something and take off, but he didn't. "It isn't only Thais I care about," he said, sounding tired. He ran one hand through his dark hair and looked at me. He was almost six feet tall, much taller than Richard. "I absolutely care about you, Clio, sincerely."

I was so taken aback I couldn't come up with an acid-etched answer.

"I met you first, and it was your beauty that first captured me," he went on in a low voice. "I love your fire and your strength. You own your body, you know how to use it. You knew what you wanted from me. You know what you want in general. That all appeals to me greatly."

I took a quick sip of my tea so I wouldn't run screaming into the woods. The worst part was, I wanted to believe him—even almost did believe him. I wanted him so much, I needed his lies to be true.

"Then you met my sister and went for the two for one?" I asked, proud of myself for my voice not wavering.

Luc winced, and I wanted to hold him, press his

head against my chest and stroke his hair and comfort him. Can we say "masochist"?

"I made a huge mistake. I treated you both unfairly and faithlessly. I'm very sorry, Clio—believe me. I never meant to hurt you. I was happy when I was with you, and I had hoped to make you happy too."

"Then you might want to try not two-timing me with my twin sister." My teeth were clenched tight, my hands curled at my sides. I was furious at him for lying, for manipulating me, and I was even more furious at myself for wanting him *anyway*.

I stalked away, trying to calm down. It was bad enough I felt this way without anyone knowing. Having it be public would be more than I could bear.

Nan and Thais were setting up the large circle, helped by Manon and Jules. Daedalus seemed to be reading from a large, old book. Sophie and Ouida were talking, their arms full of leafy branches. Axelle was at another table, putting a piece of cheese on a cracker. Everyone was busy—I could take a minute to get a grip. I ducked into the woods and almost immediately yelped when someone grabbed me.

"What do *you* want?" I sputtered, yanking my arm out of Richard's grasp.

"I don't know," he said, frowning. "I don't know."

Then, before I could say a word, his head came down and his mouth was on mine. He leaned against me with enough force to push me back a foot against the broad trunk of a live oak. My eyes opened wide in surprise, and then his arms were around me, protecting my bare back from the rough tree bark. He slanted his head a different way to kiss me more deeply, and still I hadn't reacted, hadn't pushed him away, wasn't even kissing him back.

All I could think was, *He just* said *he wouldn't do this again.*

And, *He said he hadn't meant it.*

And, *Luc was just yanking my chain. He loves Thais.*

Finally, *This . . . feels . . . good.*

I put my hands out and gripped Richard's upper arms, thinking, *I've got to get out of here.* Then every thought I had just evaporated. My eyes slowly shut and my whole body relaxed, pressed between him and the tree. His arms were smooth and hard under my hands, his skin warm. I opened my mouth and kissed him back, felt his surprise, his body tighten. My hands slid up his shoulders and held him more closely against me, one hand keeping his head in place.

I was so heartsore over Luc, over everything that had happened. It felt so wonderful to feel good again, just for a minute.

Suddenly Richard broke the kiss, leaving me gasping. "Say my name," he said, breathing hard while I blinked stupidly at him. "Say my name."

"Richard," I said breathlessly. "*Ree*-shard."

He kissed me again, harder, and I gave up completely, pressing myself against him, feeling his lithe hardness, his smooth, wiry muscles. The cloth of his robe was soft and thin, and our bodies felt so close. Richard was more my size, fit easily into my arms, against my body. He pushed one knee between mine, pressing my *bouvre* back against my legs.

I heard myself making little sounds, hungry sounds I'd heard before, and I thought, *I want him.*

"Clio? Clio!"

Someone was calling me. Nan. I pushed Richard away. We stared at each other, panting, my hands on his shoulders, his around my waist.

"Thais, go find Clio, will you?" I heard Nan ask.

"Oh God!" I whispered. I whipped my hands away from him as if electrified. "God!"

Richard stepped back from me, his face flushed, hunger in his eyes. He looked as shocked as I felt.

"I—damn it," he said, breathing hard, sounding appalled. "I didn't—"

I just stared at him, unable to process what I had been doing.

I turned and walked quickly away, smoothing my hair with my hands. I tugged down on the skirt of my gown, feeling limp and overheated. When I was closer to the tables, I came back out of the woods.

"Nan?" I called, striving for normalcy. "Did you want me?"

She turned at the sound of my voice. I saw that the other members of the Treize were gathering in the circle. The sun was setting; it was time to begin. I took off my shoes and walked barefoot through the grass, not looking at Luc. On the opposite side of the woods, Richard came out into the clearing. He carefully didn't look at me, and I didn't look at him.

It was hot and sticky, as usual. Clio's face was flushed and pink from the heat, and I guessed that I looked the same. The circle was forming; people were gathering. Luc walked over from the tables, and Richard came out of the woods across the clearing. I wanted to be next to Clio or Petra or Ouida, but people started linking hands, and I ended up between Jules and Richard. After Jules, there was Sophie, Daedalus, Petra, Manon, then Clio. On Clio's other side was Axelle, then Luc, and finally Ouida, on Richard's other side. Richard's hand was warm and dry, his fingers firm and strong.

I glanced at Clio, and she gave me a little smile. She looked upset or tense, and I figured seeing Luc again was throwing her off. I actually felt weirdly calm and confident. I finally knew what my element was, and this was the first time I would make "big" magick with that knowledge. I hoped I would feel magick coming alive inside me. It was a little scary, but Petra and Ouida were here, and somehow they made me feel safe.

"Friends," Daedalus began, "our journey to this

point has been unexpected and harder than we could have known. Yet how glad I am to share this Récolte celebration with you, the people I have known longest, the people I grew up with. And how glad I am to welcome Clio and Thais to our circle."

He smiled and nodded at both of us, and Ouida smiled at us encouragingly. As Daedalus went on, I remembered to calm my breathing and release any lingering tension inside me. Luc—I just had to let it go. I rolled my shoulders and breathed out, counting to four, and then breathed in, counting to four. I tried to clear my mind of everything around me and open it to everything I could receive from everyone else.

Slowly we started moving clockwise in our circle. The sun would set in another three or four minutes—it was deep twilight, and the woods behind me were black.

I closed my eyes and listened as Daedalus started the chant. I'd never heard it before, but Petra had told me that each sabbat had its own traditions, songs, and foods, just like with Christianity or any other religion. I liked how the *Bonne Magie* emphasized having a cycle, with no beginning and no end. Everything we did here tonight could be done next year at Récolte. Everyone around me had done almost exactly this at every other Récolte they'd celebrated throughout their lives. And after this, the next holiday was Monvoile, which came on Halloween, and then Soliver at the winter solstice. The sun rose and set, the seasons bloomed and died, everything was a circle, an unending rhythm. I'd never thought about life like that, and I really liked it. It gave a sort of structure and sense of permanence to my confusing, impermanent life.

All at once I realized that the Treize itself was unnatural, out of cycle. These people had been born and should have lived and then died, their natural cycle. Then they would have been born again, and their souls would have another lifetime to try to improve and advance farther on their path, according to their beliefs, as Petra had explained them to me.

But the Treize hadn't died. They'd been born but become stuck in a static, linear life. How weird. Was it having some effect? Like, on their souls or even on the world around them? I didn't know—didn't even know if I believed all that.

Next to me, Jules's beautiful, deep voice started to weave in and out in the chant. Most people were singing now. I didn't have my own personal song, but I just closed my eyes and thought about water, my element, and everything it meant to me. Then I opened my mouth and let whatever came to me become a sound.

At first I sang very softly, not wanting to mess anyone else up if I was doing it wrong. But I felt like I was actually singing a song and not just making a bunch of unconnected sounds. It felt like there was a song already written inside me that I was letting out. It felt good, and natural. I let my voice join the others lightly, following them without trying to be louder or alone, just blending. Slowly, as I concentrated, faint impressions came to me.

I focused on opening my senses, and gradually I was able to separate out emotions and people. I almost caught my breath—it was incredible. I could actually feel that Manon was unhappy and that she also felt guilty. About what? And Daedalus was already sending out waves of triumph, as though some goal had been achieved. That was creepy.

I tried deliberately reaching out to Sophie, just to see what would happen. To my surprise, I was hit with a wave of sadness that was so strong I opened my eyes. Her face looked impassive, the same as always, but her large brown eyes were haunted, and I felt a sense of desperation—almost steely resolve. To do what?

From Ouida, I felt calm, radiating peace and love—what a relief. She felt wary but was concentrating on sending out only good. Thank heavens. Then there was Luc. I couldn't help it—I opened my eyes and shot a quick glance at him. His eyes were closed; he was singing, joining in with the others. I felt a deep wave of remorse and longing coming from him. He was so beautiful, so haunted in the deepening twilight. Suddenly I was fiercely glad that he was there, that we were both part of making magick, no matter how far apart we were. With no warning, I felt a powerful rush of love and sad desire for him. I tried to squelch it immediately, but it was too late. He felt it. His eyes popped open and he stared at me. Quickly I looked away, swallowing my feelings, but my eyes caught Clio's. She'd been watching Luc. She'd seen us looking at each other. Miserably I wondered if she'd felt my emotions. I hoped not. Deliberately I closed my eyes and cleared my mind again. I held Jules's and Richard's hands firmly, our feet doing a grapevine to the left endlessly, over and over.

Okay, Axelle now. Mostly I got a sense of impatient irritation.

Richard, right next to me, felt more closed off, as if he was concentrating on not sending out anything. What little I picked up felt like confusion, anger, doubt.

I opened my eyes a slit and looked at Clio again. Her eyes were closed, her face flushed and damp. She looked . . . beautiful. Did that mean I did too?

Relax. Concentrate. In the middle of the circle a small fire burned. Near it, at the four points of the compass, were thick gold pillar candles inside tall hurricane-glass holders two feet high. The fire was ringed with stones, and between the candles were stone bowls of water. I let myself feel each element, concentrating on water—cool, flowing, powerful, endless, timeless. I let my voice grow stronger. Our circle was moving more swiftly now. Petra had explained that the Récolte song had once had actual words, but that they'd been lost over the centuries. It seemed so odd that this had been going on for centuries and until now, I hadn't ever heard about it. But the song had once praised the earth for growing people's food, praised the sun for keeping everything alive, and praised rain for nourishing them as well as their crops. It was all about how the earth had given to them and they had taken. Next spring, they would give back to the earth when they planted things and enriched the soil. It was about the promise of returning life in return for the life they had received.

It was a haunting, beautiful, otherworldly-sounding song, and I felt weirdly emotional and thankful for everything I had. I'd lost so much, and after losing my father I hadn't been able to imagine ever feeling close to whole again. But now with Clio and Petra, I had a family again. And even more than that—I had a connection to this deep magick within me. It had terrified me at first, but now . . . now that I was finally feeling close to it, close to *myself,* it was like a door had opened to another entire part of my life.

Suddenly I began to feel a strong thread twisting through the woven song. I realized the energy of the circle felt off balance, discordant. There was anger in the thread, and it was coloring our magick dark. I opened my eyes and looked at Petra, who was facing straight ahead, her chin firm as she sang. She felt it too. Glancing at Clio, I saw that she looked puzzled, concerned. I kept singing, not knowing what else to do or what was going on.

I realized I was caught up in magick—it was overwhelming, stronger than me, stronger than anything I had felt before. I looked from face to face, but everything was a blur, a dizzying swirl of light and color and sound. I saw Clio staring at Luc, then turning away. I saw Ouida nod at Petra. Richard, next to me, was watching Daedalus, frowning, and when I looked at Daedalus, I recognized the source of the dark magick.

Daedalus was using our energy to work some other spell. I wanted to break out of the circle but didn't know how, didn't think I could. I was hot, burning up, damp with heat, and my throat was dry and sore.

I closed my eyes for a second, starting to feel sick, and when I opened them, I saw Petra nod at Ouida and Luc. Suddenly she wrenched her hand out of mine. The three of them threw their hands up, shouting words I didn't recognize, and it was like the world had been pulled out from under us. Jules and I, still holding hands, stumbled and started to fall, and then with no warning the big glass flutes shielding the candles burst.

"Oh!" I cried, feeling my cheek and shoulder sting, and then I fell hard to the ground and felt the world sway beneath me.

Other people fell around me, crying out. Daedalus's voice was choked with rage, and then all was still and quiet. I felt terrible, nauseated. My head throbbed and my forehead stung, maybe from getting hit by flying glass. My eyes filled with tears.

"Thais." Painfully I turned my head to see that Clio had crawled over to me. Her face was unnaturally white, with greenish edges. Her shoulders were scratched and bleeding. "Are you okay?" she asked, and then she simply collapsed on the ground next to me. I reached out and felt her hand, her fingers closing around mine.

"I'm gonna barf," I croaked, starting to cry. "What happened? Did I do that?"

"No, no," she said weakly. "Nan and Ouida ended the circle unnaturally. You always have to bring a circle down slowly, the way it began, and finish it properly. If you don't, you feel like this."

"It feels horrible," I said, sounding like a baby. "Why did they do it?"

"I think Daedalus was doing something," she said.

I put my hand to my cheek. Blood trickled down the side of my face to the ground. My arms were cut in several places.

"I think he was working dark magick, using the circle," Clio went on, her voice breaking. "Nan and Ouida broke it to stop him."

My face crumpled and tears slid down my cheeks. "Was he trying to hurt us, you and me?"

She held my hand more tightly. "I don't know. But it's okay," she said. "We're fine. I'm here, and Nan is here."

"Girls?" Petra leaned over us, her face ashen. "Are you all right?"

"No," I said, starting to cry more. I remembered how excited I'd been to start the circle, how thrilling it had been, feeling the magick rise. Now I felt naive and stupid, duped. "I never want to do this again."

"I'm sorry, darling," said Petra, sitting by us. She reached out and put a hand on each of us. "I'm so sorry. It really isn't usually like this. Ouida, Luc, and I had to try to stop Daedalus."

"But you didn't, you know," said Daedalus, sounding wheezy but triumphant. Like I'd felt him before. "It succeeded."

"What were you *doing?*" Jules sounded furious.

With difficulty, I propped myself up enough to see that the others were in various stages of recovery. Manon was crying also, and Sophie was holding her, kissing her face. Axelle was leaning over into some bushes, being sick. Luc and Richard got up, and they both looked as furious as Jules sounded. Luc was pale and clammy, his deep green *bouvre* dark with sweat. Like the rest of us, Luc was cut all over from when the glass burst. Thin ribbons of blood trailed down his face and arms.

"A forceful summoning." Daedalus sounded so pleased with himself that I wanted to kick him. "For Marcel and Claire. There's no way they can resist coming now. I'll have my Treize."

"You fricking jerk!" Clio choked out, sitting up. "How dare you—?"

He turned to her, his eyes like ice. "I dare much, little girl," he said. "And you'll thank me before this is through."

"Get up." Luc glared down at Daedalus.

"Oh, Luc, really," Daedalus said. He got to his feet a little shakily, and as soon as he was up, Luc swung back and punched him so hard it knocked Daedalus off his feet.

Daedalus lay still on his back, his mouth gasping like a fish.

"Get up," Luc said again, and spit blood onto the ground.

Ouida came over, moving stiffly. "Please, Luc, don't," she said, putting a hand on his arm. He ignored her for a moment, then turned to her. His chest was heaving and his eyes gleamed with anger. "I'm asking you," she said more softly. "Please."

After several long moments, Luc swallowed and stepped back but glared down at Daedalus.

Richard came over, his upper lip cut, his robe sliced in several blood-rimmed places. He looked down at Daedalus.

"Try it again, old man," he said, his voice still and deadly. "Try using me again like that against my will and I'll find a way to kill you. I promise."

Daedalus looked shocked. "Riche—" he began, but Richard had already turned and walked away, heading to the food tables.

I lay back down, feeling better as soon as I was touching the earth from head to foot. I looked up at Petra.

"Can we get out of here?"

"Yes," she said firmly. "As soon as you two can walk."

Hurricane Force

What was this guy's name? Pak? Pakpao? Whatever. Claire lifted her hair off her neck and fell over sideways on the bed.

The guy said something to her, but the only word Claire caught was *beautiful*.

She smiled and patted his arm sleepily. "Yeah, yeah."

In the next instant, the finely carved wooden screens on her windows blew inward with hurricane force. Empty bottles fell and smashed on the ground. The single lightbulb overhead burst, showering Claire with hot, fine pieces of glass.

The magick hit Claire in the chest like a fist, and she bolted upright, gasping.

Daedalus! That bastard! Claire sprang out of bed, swearing furiously. Pak was frightened, chattering in Thai, something about a storm. She ignored him, stomping around her room. Her feet were cut by the broken glass, but she ignored that too. Damn Daedalus! Picking up a heavy brass incense holder, Claire hurled it against the wall. It knocked a chip out of the plaster and fell to the floor with a crunching sound. She would kill him—somehow she would find a way. She would absolutely cut out his beating heart. Had anyone ever tried that?

Finally Claire sank back down on the bed. Pak put his hand on her shoulder, concerned. She shrugged him off, told him to leave now. At least she'd learned that much Thai. Very useful. While the guy, completely bewildered, got dressed, Claire hung her head, so angry she could hardly breathe. A liquor bottle had broken near her foot, and the sticky puddle touched her bare foot. The alcohol burned her cuts, but none of it mattered.

Pak tried to talk to her once again, but she waved him away. She wouldn't cry—Claire never cried, but she almost wished she could right now. In a few moments she had to get up, throw some things together, and grab a taxi to the airport. She was going to New Orleans. And once she was there, she was going to make sure that Daedalus understood he was never, ever to mess with her again.

A Spell of Forceful Summoning

Marcel was dreaming. In his dream, he was tending a garden by a river, back in Louisiana. There was water everywhere in Louisiana, rivers everywhere, like the canals in Amsterdam. When he was young, people had used the rivers much more than the rutted, muddy roads.

There were two kinds of rivers. One kind was opaque and green, with warm, slow-moving water. The other kind was clear and red-tinged, with cold water that moved fast. They were both good to swim in, drink from, catch fish in. Here in Ireland, despite the very different climate, Marcel had lots of seafood, like back home. Crabs and shrimp, all different kinds of fish. He loved that about Ireland, the greenness, the water. Like home.

In his dream, Marcel was tending a garden. Looking up, he saw a lone pirogue moving slowly down the river. It must have broken loose from somewhere. Marcel made his way down the slippery clay bank, avoiding the knobby cypress knees poking up through the water. He grabbed a long branch and hooked it on one end of the little flat-bottomed boat.

He would pull it to shore and tie it up, find out whose it was.

The pirogue bumped against roots, its bottom scraping the shore. Marcel leaned down to grab its trailing rope, then stopped, frozen. Inside the boat was a body. His breath caught in his throat as he pulled the boat closer. It was a girl, not yet twenty. She lay peacefully on the boat's floor, eyes closed, arms crossed over her chest. She looked like she was sleeping except for the unnatural pallor of her skin, her blue-tinged lips and fingertips.

Now he saw that she was wet, her dress sodden and clinging to her, her black hair streaming back. Cerise's birthmark burned on her cheekbone, bright red.

Cerise? No—of course not. Cerise had been blond. But this girl looked just like Cerise, if Cerise had had black hair. And this girl had drowned. Cerise had died in childbirth.

Who was she? Marcel reached out one shaking hand—and then the small, high window of his monk's cell burst inward, the shards of glass streaking across his face and hands, leaving fine red lines.

Marcel shot up, cold sweat breaking out instantly. His room was pitch dark; his window was shattered. Icy air rolled in through the small opening, pooling and settling all around him. His heart was pounding, and then it hit him: the knowledge of what this was, what Daedalus had done.

"Oh God." Marcel moaned and pressed his hands against his face, feeling the warm stickiness of his blood. Bits of glass stung him, but it didn't matter. Daedalus had thrown a thick velvet rope around his neck, all the way from America. Now he was going to pull it in, and there was nothing Marcel could do about it. Everything in him was urging him to America. He felt like if he didn't get there as soon as possible, his skin would erupt and spiders would swarm all over his body. He had to get there fast, fast, fast.

That was what a spell of forceful summoning felt like. It made you panic, made every second's delay feel like torture. He would feel like he had the plague until he set foot in Louisiana again.

Marcel hung his head, biting back bitter tears. He wasn't strong enough to resist this spell. If he was truly worthy, he would be able to reject it, to pray his way out of it, work harder against it.

But he wasn't worthy. He'd always known that.

Stifling a sob in his throat, Marcel began to review what needed to be done. Not much. Just getting up, telling Father Jonah that he must leave, and making his way to the Shannon airport. Oh God. He would see them all again. Daedalus, who had done this to him. Petra, whom he loved but also feared. Richard, his mortal enemy, who had killed Cerise. Manon, with whom he shared a terrible secret. And so on. All of them.

He didn't need to know why Daedalus had summoned him to New Orleans. He already knew what awaited him there: pain and destruction. And the absolute end of any hope he had of his salvation.